THE SMALL ICY VILLAGE OF GATSBAHLBURG

THE SMALL ICY VILLAGE OF GATSBAHLBURG

and the Blossom of an Ocean

B.A.D.

Copyright © 2022 B.A.D.

All rights reserved.

TABLE OF CONTENTS

Chapter I	This Tiny Village of Mine	1
Chapter II	A Normal Day in Gatsbahlburg	13
Chapter III	Blood Drawn at the Gathering-Pit	41
Chapter IV	A Prophecy Fulfilled	59
Chapter V	The Arrival of More Eyes	78
Chapter VI	My Last Birthday in Gatsbahlburg	98
Chapter VII	Goodbye and Good Luck, My Dear Brave Friends	122
Chapter VIII	Their Surprising Return, and Mysteries Unveiled	131
Chapter IX	Gatsbahlburg Changed Forever	165
Chapter X	Decision Day, the End, and From Where I Tell You This Story	174

Chapter I

THIS TINY VILLAGE OF MINE

My name is Hans Strasburg, I am fourteen years old, and I live in the lonely village of Gatsbahlburg.

For a time, I didn't know much about the rest of the world, if there *was* a world, or what life might have been like outside of my village.

But this place... *this* village, my home... I know very well.

I can tell you all about it, actually. Everything about it: from the village itself, and the customs it holds; to the layout within it, and the environment which surrounds it; about the life inside of it, and the lack of life outside of it; all the way to the people who live here... and the people who rule here.

In fact, I think I'll do just that.

There's a story I have that I wish to tell you, and knowing every detail about my home will greatly aid in its delivery.

You see, this story became something so much more than just another strange existence or the simple undertaking of an experience through life, because of the way it ends and where I came to be at its conclusion. If it hadn't been for that, then myself *and* this story would've just been another passing of existence— with not much meaning, truth, or power to be taken away from it.

Though I am telling you all this from the end of my story, I will do my best to keep it all in the original perspective from when it was first occurring. So much more is now within my capacity of understanding, that retelling you this story in such a simple manner should prove an easy enough task.

However, I must remark that I was thirteen at the beginning of this story, and fourteen at the end of it— just to clear up any possible confusion.

But with that being said, allow me to begin the telling of this great tale for you, one which touched all of our lives within the small icy village of Gatsbahlburg.

And to start it, I will describe this home of mine.

Snow, Cold, Ice, and the Ocean— these four things make up the land which we live on and that which surrounds us.

On the thickest, largest, and most dense slab of ice which never has and never will melt, sits Gatsbahlburg.

The great ocean surrounds us as a never ending glistening sea of frigid waters, that twinkles with the gentlest of currents which are forever in a constant motion. Sometimes, certain parts of the ocean will freeze over, but with time or by force, they eventually

THE SMALL ICY VILLAGE OF GATSBAHLBURG

break— unlike the frozen slab that eternally holds strong and acts as Gatsbahlburg's foundation.

Gatsbahlburg itself is as large as it is small. Only a couple hundred people live in the village. Most are adults, few are older, and even fewer are children. It's a tight-knit community that contains everything it needs for life and a stable existence in the simplest of forms.

At the center of the village lies a large pond, and in the center of that pond is an even smaller foundation that bears the Four Fruit trees.

These Four Fruit trees are like brothers and sisters, where they almost look the same and are obviously related, but are also undeniably their own individuals at the end of the day, and therefore, all produce different fruit.

The First Fruit we use for eating— to give us life.

The Second Fruit we use to make candles— to light our path in the dark.

The Third Fruit we use for healing— to mend our broken bodies.

And the Fourth Fruit we use to make spirits— so that we may have joy in this life.

Besides the pond, two more open bodies of water exist within the foundation's structure.

There's the Grove— a large open section of broken ice that forms a crescent moon shape around almost half of the foundation's outskirt. And then there's the Isle, which lies on the opposing outskirt of the Grove, all the way across the village on its other end.

At the Grove, my friends and I like to sit on the broken ice slabs and push ourselves further out, towards the center of the open water, where we can hold private conversations with each other.

The Isle is the more popular place for my peers to hangout at, as its open plane of water is much slimmer and not nearly as big as the Grove's— in fact, it would take only three children shoulder to shoulder to bridge the gap of its width... though its length reaches all the way down to Gatsbahlburg's entrance.

Large snow mounds that have hardened over time act as an insulating wall which contains our community from the edge of the foundation— except for the entrance, of course, as the snow stops at the two wooden posts that hold up the arching sign containing our name.

Everything else that exists here was created by the first residents who settled on this great slab of ice. Currently, we still occupy those wooden structures that were built long ago by our ancestors, and have remained intact all of these years later for our own use... as there is no more wood to build with any more.

These wooden structures include:

The homes for the families— all clustered together near the entrance of Gatsbahlburg.

The Spirit Workshop and the Candle Workshop— housing the production of the spirits we drink and the candles which light up our lives.

The school house— which serves as both a place for the youth to learn, as well as the Council's courthouse.

And the Gathering-Pit— which is built like a small colosseum and where we hold the tradition of the Gathering-Pit performance.

In regards to the school, our education starts when we turn five and consists of learning about the history and culture of our village; understanding why we have the traditions that we perform; the customs we must learn; the process of creating the spirits we drink and the candles we light; the value of community and our Four Fruit trees; and most importantly, the Prophecy that our ancestors left us with.

The Gathering-Pit is where the whole community will come together, four times each year, and watch the youth put on a semi-choreographed performance while passages from our Prophecy is recited by the Council. We use real weapons and put our hearts into the performance— as instructed by the Council and per tradition —so injuries are extremely common… and some fatalities have been known to occur.

Though minor in comparison to these buildings and houses, that last pieces of wooden structure crafted by our ancestors, stand at the entrance to our village and consists of two things; the great wooden sign that bears our home's name which one must walk under to enter or leave our community; and the giant wooden totem placed directly beneath it, decorated with carvings that are related to the Prophecy.

It should also be noted that only two seasons exist here: Day Breaker and Night Wafter. And these seasons contribute major aspects or possibilities to our lives.

Day Breaker lasts for half of the year, starting at its beginning and ending in its middle. During Day Breaker, snowfall is scarce despite it still being cold outside. The sun rises early, and sets late. The ocean glistens endlessly from experiencing the most sunlight during the day, which in turn, results in little to no ice freezing on its surface— and whatever slabs do manage to form during Day Breaker are consistently weak and brittle, easily able to be broken apart during this time.

Night Wafter lasts for the other half of the year, starting in its middle and continuing 'till its end. During Night Wafter, snow will never stop falling down from the sky, but the pace by which it descends is slow and almost weightless— like gravity barely exists. The sun rises late, and sets early, and many ice slabs form on the ocean's surface during this time, strong and sturdy, especially outside the village's foundation.

… I might have given you more information about my home than is necessary, and I apologize for that.

It is easy for me to get lost in the details, as this was once all I ever knew. But allow me to get back on track, for there are two very important pieces to the puzzle that is my story which you must be aware of.

The Council… and the Prophecy.

The Council is a group of old men, usually around four to six of them, who are in charge of our village.

Of course, there's not much to be in charge of— for it is simple living here. But… there are still some things that are decided by the Council's voice.

THE SMALL ICY VILLAGE OF GATSBAHLBURG

Such as the distributed responsibilities for the making of the spirits or candles. To keep efficiency, a schedule and assigned duties are given out for these two crafts, as they are very important and essential for our way of life here.

Another power held by the Council, is getting to select the teacher who will take on the responsibility of passing down the traditions and knowledge of Gatsbahlburg unto the youth.

The Council are also the ones who get to choose the next or future members that will replace them when their old bodies wither away.

But the greatest power the Council holds, is the deciding on who will stay and who will be forced to leave when the youth turns of age and must find a partner to have children of their own with.

Truth is— we aren't the only snowy village on a strong platform of unfreezing ice.

There are others.

However, to our knowledge, there are only a few and they are very far away. The journey to the other villages can be made only during Night Wafter, when the cold has reached its peak and there are plenty of strong ice slabs to trek atop over the great ocean. And even then, there's no guarantee that they will hold firm enough for the entirety of your journey, or if the next step you take will break and be your last.

… I wish I could talk more about the other villages— what they're like; what their people are like; what they might look like; the similarities and differences between us; their history and traditions, and perhaps even their own prophecies that have been passed down by their ancestors... but I cannot.

The reason I cannot, is because the Council also creates the rules which we must abide by... and one of them is the solitude in only knowing knowledge that pertains to our village, Gatsbahlburg. That is all we are allowed to be taught about. That is all we are allowed to know.

For one to ever find out anything regarding the other villages, would be by being chosen to leave Gatsbahlburg in the pursuit of a partner, and only if you are successful and survive the journey... well, then you'll probably learn everything about your new home once it's reached.

Around the same time when young adults of our own are sent off on their journey across the great ocean, we too, often receive some newcomers of age who have traveled out of their villages to find partners in marriage to mate with.

But these newcomers never tell us about their village, their original homes, their customs or what their life was once like— for it is forbidden. And now being residents of Gatsbahlburg, they must obey the rules that have been put in place by the Council.

And whether it's the same where they live, and so they expected nothing less; or because the travel here was so long, and hard, and riddle with so much possible death, that they refuse to be sent back out onto the ice; or maybe because they find this rule easy to accept compared to what could've been taking place at their previous village... the newcomers accept it and keep their mouths shut on their pasts, while picking up the traditions and lifestyle of Gatsbahlburg.

There's only one other forbidden action within our village, and that is to never enter the waters of the Ocean— including the openings that sit within our home such as the Grove, the Isle, or the pond surrounding the Four Fruit trees.

Now, for the Prophecy.

The Prophecy is a mysterious yet vital part of Gatsbahlburg, this story, and even the Council since their whole existence relies upon it.

The Prophecy speaks in correlation to our beginning, and the Council ties into because of our supposed end.

Though the Prophecy speaks in a strange manner which you'd expect from an old script written by the enigmatic tongue that was once upon a knowing— I think I'll give you the bare-bone version of it now, and the full version of it, in its proper form, at the end of my story.

It didn't make much sense to me for the majority of my life, and it only became clear once I achieved this state from which I am delivering this story to you now. After my telling of this story, I believe we'll both share an understanding of its ancient words, from the new perspective that will be gained.

The Prophecy speaks of a being with Blue eyes who shall make its return to our village in the future— when the time of a new pilgrimage has arrived. This being with Blue eyes will then choose the new leader of Gatsbahlburg, who will set unto handling and reconstructing our little world here, as did our first leader when our ancestors arrived at this icy foundation and made it our home at the beginning of time.

But until then, until the Prophecy comes into fruition, we are to live the life our ancestors wanted for themselves and for us when they first came here— happy, fulfilled, and simple.

The Council took power many years ago. So long ago in fact, that their "necessary presence" became written into our history. They say we need the order and structure they provide for us until the being with Blue eyes arrives, otherwise we may fail ourselves before we can ever see the Blue eyed being's arrival.

However, the Council has always promised to step down from their appointed positions of power when the Blue eyed being comes, and declared that they would willing hand off their rule over Gatsbahlburg to the chosen one, since "it is only right that the Prophecy be respected and played out in the order of its natural law".

Almost everyone in Gatsbahlburg has no problem with this or the Council, because in all honesty, our lives do go on the same while they're in power.

And now, it's more of a wonder of what *could* happen should they not be there at this point. For perhaps harm *may* find its way into our lives by some misfortune should the Council not be in place…

Having said all of this, I believe I can start my story now. So without further or do, allow me to enlighten you.

We'll start at the beginning.

Not the absolute beginning with my birth or anything like that, but the beginning of when everything began to change... or perhaps... a couple steps back from then— the few moments and days of life before that great change arrived.

Chapter II

A NORMAL DAY IN GATSBAHLBURG

Ma and Pa woke me early in the morning by their soft voices filled with love, along with the scent of the First Fruit cooking in the kitchen.

It was colder today despite Night Wafter nearing its end, and Day Breaker being just around the corner. And although the snow had lessened in its heavy fall, the wind kept its temperature in a ruthless manner.

I got out of bed and put on all the layers I had, which were extra snug and warm since I was close to outgrowing them, meaning that I would soon be given the next size up of a clothing collection while also handing down mine to someone who was younger and more fitting.

Once I was all put together for the day ahead of me, I met with my parents in the kitchen, where we sat down together and shared our first meal of the day.

"Your birthday's getting close" said Pa in-between bites of the sloshy reduced porridge of First Fruit, still steaming from coming fresh out the cauldron, "That means you only have one more year of school left!

Excited?" he asked.

I shrugged and stirred my bowl in an attempt to let its contents cool before eating, "Yeah, I guess" I answered, "It'll be nice to hangout with Dan again on a full-day basis. And also to not have to worry about the Gathering-Pit performances or getting hurt from a possible accident."

"Dan?" inquired Ma, "Does that mean you're hoping to be assigned Spirit Making once you finish school?" she asked.

I nodded, "It would be nice if me and him shared the same workshop, but either way, we'll have more time to hangout like we used to once I'm out of school.

But Dan did say he enjoyed Spirit Making, so I guess that's a plus too at the thought of it."

"Most usually hope to be assigned to Spirit Making" said Pa, "And I'll admit, I had the same hope of it when I was your age— I mean, who doesn't love spirits?

But I'll tell you, the Second Fruit is such a fascinating thing! I grew to love and appreciate it far more than the spirit once I learned more about the fruit and how to craft candles from it when I was assigned to Light Crafting.

There's a lot more to it than you'd think" he continued, "The quality of the burn; the size of the flame; the tame of the flicker; the duration of its shine— all of these varying aspects I never once took notice of, nor even realized were changeable factors, until I began my learning in the workshop."

"And I can say the same for Spirit Making!" countered Ma, full of glee, "Dan and I have different work schedules, so I haven't encountered him while on my hours. But I'm certain he's learning about all of the variables that go into Spirit Making, and just how many varieties can be brewed up by the different preparations concocted of the Fourth Fruit!

So, you'll have just as much fun and growth in knowledge if that's what you're assigned as well!"

"Well… there's always a chance I won't be working at either of the workshops for too long" I said while taking my first couple bites of the porridge, "I might be selected to leave the village when I come of age. That means I'll only be in a workshop for three years before I go."

My parents halted their eating and looked at each other.

"Have you… thought about leaving here?" asked Pa.

I shrugged again, "I know it's a possibility, so I've never ruled it out from happening."

"… Do you want to leave here?" asked Ma.

"I don't know" I answered honestly, "I do love my home here, and my friends, and of course— my family. But I guess I've always been curious about the other villages.

I know we're not allowed to talk about it or ask the newcomers about their previous homes. But that doesn't make them not exist… aren't you even the slightest bit curious?" I asked.

Pa shook his head, "This is our home" he said bluntly, "Why would I care about anything outside of it?

It doesn't matter what the other villages are like, or its life, or its people.

I couldn't care less about their history, or their customs, or their qualities and characteristics.

I live *here*, as do you and your mother. What more is there to regard in being or living outside of here, if outside is never where we go?" he challenged.

"That's what curiosity is though, Pa" I answered back, "Because of *exactly* that."

Ma must've picked up on the defeated tone in my voice—although I would've argued it was one more of a fruitless exhaustion —as she promptly responded with, "Your Pa and I were born here and have stayed here all our lives.

We're *true* natives of Gatsbahlburg.

There's not a chance that exists anymore of your father or I leaving here. This will be the place where our bodies grow old, die, and eventually be set free into the ocean in the ceremony after passing.

For us, Hans, such thoughts are irrelevant and don't contribute much to our lives.

Yes— there is a chance you may be selected to leave this village when you come of age... but curiosity aside... is that something you truly desire?

Think about it fully.

It means goodbye to me, goodbye to Pa, goodbye to your friends— goodbye to everything you know and love here.

There's no guarantee that the other villages will even have fruit trees:

You may have to eat something strange that you do not like for the rest of your life.

They may not make spirits, and you'll never have such a drink to warm your belly and body in the cold, nor alleviate your mood into wistful joy.

They may not craft candles. And after the falling of the sun, it may be eternally dark until it rises again in the morning.

They may not have the ability to heal and mend wounds, and you may be forced to bear any pain or injury you acquire until your body heals itself, or the cold numbs the sensation.

They might have rules, customs, and ceremonies that you are uncomfortable with— which you'll now have to endure until your own passing."

"You said at the beginning of this conversation that you were relieved to be nearing the end of your participation in the Gathering-Pit performances" added Pa, "What if the other villages have similar events but with no age caps on them, and you are forced to participate every year at any age?

What if they have something even more dangerous with an even higher risk of injury or death as part of their own tradition?

What if they have certain customs and practices that are only applied to *their* newcomers?

Imagine that, now.

We are quite kind in the perspective that we only require the newcomers to abandon everything from their past and assimilate to their new lives here.

And though they may not be allowed to talk about their pasts, there's no rule in place that prevents them from complaining. When was the last time you heard someone from a different village ever complain about their life in Gatsbahlburg?"

Mother smiled and nodded her head in agreement, glancing from Pa to me.

A tiny heartbeat within me gave a single flaring pump that rushed throughout my body. Like the gentlest flicker from a candle that lights up the night of our village and brightens the space around it— so too, for a brief moment, did defiance fill my internal being at my parents' nature of rebuttal.

But I lacked the spine to properly deliver that fire which brewed within me, and instead, chose to voice my disagreement and hurt from their tossing of my opinion, by pointing out the insensitivities of their words, "Well... if I am selected to leave here when I come of age, I now have your perspectives to haunt my thoughts as I trek the frozen slabs across the ocean" I said, "Something which you both already admitted to as being an event you no longer need to concern yourselves with."

Ma and Pa's reaction to what I said were that of surprise and regret, only realizing in this moment now how their words carried more persecution than reflection, leaving them at a loss in how to properly respond.

Their expressions resembled a similar look to as if they had slightly choked on their First Fruit— uncomfortable, embarrassed, and awkward.

After a long silence had passed, one which contained many glances between Ma and Pa to each other in an unspoken conversation between their eyes, Pa finally broke the still air at the table.

"You… don't have to worry about leaving the village, Hans" he said.

"We didn't mean to be heartless or to set fear in you at the possibility of being selected. We just already knew such a thing was never going to happen… which is why we spoke so harshly and freely at the prospect" admitted Ma.

"What do you mean?" I asked, not understanding where their confidence came from in regard to my possible selection for when I came of age.

"As you know" began Pa, "Your uncle is a member of the Council. And though I shouldn't be telling you this, nor have told your Ma... there *is* something we know that comes as very good news. Something which my brother has informed me of."

Ma and Pa smiled at each other, full of pride.

"You are a prospect— or rather —a guarantee! For holding a future place in the Council when you get older!" he said with a giant grin, one which was also shared by Ma.

My face contorted from hearing this information, leaving nothing to hide the stupefied emotion I felt at the knowledge I had just received.

"What?" I asked, although for me, it was more of a statement.

"Isn't that great!" expressed Ma.

"Why am I being considered for the Council? They're old men— it's only those of grey hair who can hold a seat. I'm not even of age to find a mate yet" I said.

"They take every resident into consideration, *especially* the youth and their future potential for the position" answered Pa, "And being that we already have a blood member in place— not to mention that you come from a lineage of true natives by way of both your mother and I —you're a strong candidate!"

I didn't know what to say at the idea of being on the Council one day, so instead, I just sat there quietly while taking it all in.

"Of course, it is a big responsibility and something that will happen in a very long time from now, so there's no need for you to fret on the matter. But just know that it is for *this* reason that you needn't worry about being chosen to leave the village when the selection does come" continued Pa, "Just live your life; love your mate when you meet her; be diligent in the workshop that you are assigned; and rest easy knowing that one day you will be on the Council when the hair on your head turns grey.

The way you currently see the village and yourself will undoubtedly change over time, and you have many years to sit with this fact. I expect you'll come to grow excited at the idea of this, like your Ma and I are about it, as you come closer to the event of it happening.

Your Ma only knows how much I would've loved to have had a seat in the Council if I could…"

Ma reached her hand out and placed it over mine, "But we've taken this morning's conversation too far into the future. For now, you still have school" she said, "Go on and walk with Talla. If this still eats at your mind throughout the day, then we can discuss it further over dinner. Okay?"

I nodded and forced a smile, then got up from my seat and left the house.

Once outside, I was hit with the early morning freeze that rushes over the foundation each day while the sun is still on its ascent. I quickly snuggled my hands into my coat pockets and kept my head down, taking this brief moment of time in the cold to go over what was just said to me at breakfast, as my feet crunched over the powdered snow while I made my way towards Talla's house.

Talla's home was only three houses down from mine, and though she was a year younger than I, we were great friends.

We always walked to school together in the morning, and being a part of my close friend group, we always hangout after school as well.

When I reached Talla's house, I knocked on her door. And after a single short pause, she was outside joining me on our routine walk to school.

It was not intentional, but I held a silence while we walked, as my mind remained in that conversation over porridge with my parents. But the silence didn't last for too long, as Talla was quick to note the difference in my behavior.

"What's going on with you?" she asked, "Did something happen?"

I shook my head, "I had a talk with my parents during breakfast that I didn't expect" I answered.

"Huh. That bad?" she asked, "What'd you do to make them angry?"

"It's not like that. They just told me something I didn't expect to hear… or anyone would expect to hear, really."

"… Aaaandd? You can't say something like that and then not tell me what they told you!"

"Well… apparently… because my uncle is on the Council, they found out that I am a prospect in holding a seat too in the future."

"That's what has you down in the dumps!?" exclaimed Talla, with a look of bewilderment on her face.

I shrugged, "It just wasn't something I expected to hear this morning."

"So!? That doesn't mean it's a bad thing just because it's a surprise! That's one of those good surprises— like finding out you've been assigned to a workshop that you were hoping to get!"

"Yeah, but it's different for you. You always speak about how you want to be on the Council when you're older. I've never really taken an interest in it or even thought about it for that matter."

"The Council governs the village" said Talla, "They keep the people and its community whole. And they make the major decisions for all of us.

It's a good thing to be a part of that and hold such a responsibility. I'd go as far as saying you're lucky for knowing about your future place in it even though it's super early.

That's my biggest dream, and I won't know if I even have a *chance* of getting a seat until my hair is grey... that's so long from now..."

"But what if you don't stay in Gatsbahlburg long enough to be a part of the Council?" I asked, "What if you're selected to leave the village when you come of age?"

Now the roles were reversed, and Talla was the one who bore a gloom at the thought of the future.

"I have thought about it... but not fondly" admitted Talla, "It's a scary thought.

I love it here— everything about this village, I hold dearly.

My dad was a newcomer when he met my mother, and though he doesn't talk about what life was like in the village where he came from, he does say that he hopes I stay in Gatsbahlburg— for the journey he made across the great ocean to get here was a hard one."

"And if the journey wasn't hard?" I asked, "Would that change your mind?"

Talla shrugged.

"Do you think more people would leave of their own free will, and venture out to the other villages, if the journey wasn't a dangerous one?" I challenged further, "Perhaps even going against the Council's decision and doing it behind their back?

My parents told me this morning that there is no reality where they will leave this village now, since they were not selected to leave when they were young and came of age.

They will die here— only ever knowing this single village amongst all of the others that exist. If the journey wasn't a hard one, I wonder if they'd then have any curiosity or inclination to leave as adults— together though —not for love or a new mate, but to enjoy the wonders of curiosity and to experience the unknown" I said.

Talla thought for a moment, genuinely considering what I had proposed before answering, "I think if the journey was not a hard one, and even if it was fairly easy, that a surprising amount of people would still choose to stay in Gatsbahlburg" she said, " And I can vouch as one of those people.

If another village was as close to us as your home is to mine, I still wouldn't want to leave here. I still wouldn't have any interest. I still would want to become a Council member when I get older" answered Talla.

I actually was caught by surprise from her answer. I had never thought of it that way before.

It never came to my mind that some people just loved Gatsbahlburg that much; that some residents truly were content with their existence here and the way things currently are; that even when offered an extended hand, or a key for easier access, or a simpler means to step into more… that some people still wouldn't care nor wish to have that curiosity answered, as it may not beat in a sync of wonder with their hearts.

"**You** should be on the Council" I said, passing a smile her way, "No one else in the village thinks like you do. You're probably the smartest person I know here.

It should honestly be you graduating in a year, and not me."

"Well if I do get a seat on the Council when my hair turns grey, I'll be sure to address this issue" she said, her voice returning to its usual confidence and proud tone, "I'll make it so that school only lasts as long as it takes you to learn the material— none of this mandatory year by year stuff until you're fifteen.

I'm only a year younger than you, and yet it's been a repetition of the same old information for the last three years. And I'm going to keep repeating it and hearing it all in class until a graduate.

It's a completely stupid system and set up that needs to change."

"What about the Gathering-Pit performances?" I asked, "Would you change that too?"

"I don't think so" said Talla, "It's tradition. It's different.

That's not to say that I'm not scared like everyone else is whenever the ceremony arrives during the year and we have to perform… but it's as much a part of this village as the Four Fruits are, and I guess its existence within our community is fated to be, since we have the Fourth Fruit for any accidents that may occur."

"Hm. Well this much I know for sure— if I do get a seat on the Council when I'm older, the Gathering-Pit performance is the **first** thing I'm getting rid of" I said.

Talla and I continued our chat as we headed to school, managing to lift each others' spirits up just by being in the other's presence.

Once we made it to class, things went about as they normally did.

We took our seats next to each other and our other friend, Lukasz.

If Dan were still in school, then our little group would've been complete, as these were the people who I always spent my time with the most.

I personally was better friends with Talla and Dan, while Lukasz was best friends with everyone, but chose to spend his time with us.

During class, our teacher, Ms. Birgit, went through the usual motions of how the schooling process went for us: teaching us segmented parts of our history in a progressional manner; revealing the lore behind our ceremonies, traditions, and their purpose; the importance of the Four Fruits, the sense of community, as well as briefly going over the natural nature of newcomers transitioning into our village during certain times of the year, as a part of the ritual for finding a mate; and what is expected from all of us as residents of Gatsbahlburg.

As you can tell— there isn't much to our school, nor what we are taught or learn.

Having started its courses and our lessons at the young age of five, most of us in attendance are fully aware of and caught up on all the material by the time we are eight. Even before school, we are fairly familiar with all of the content that would be shared with us, as we have heard it all before in small passings by our parents or through what we observe at the Gathering-Pit performances.

From eight years old until fifteen, when we are deemed finished with school by the Council, we essentially are just re-fed the same old info, stories, and lines, day in and day out.

The teacher will routinely ask questions— mainly to the younger and newer students —in order to ensure that we've been paying attention, or to gauge how much knowledge we have retained. And when the younger students fail to answer a question correctly, she will direct the same question onto one of the older students, who not only cements their successful memorization to her by knowing the right answer, but also helps out the younger student by delivering the information from a peer position.

But in general, participation from either myself or any other older counterpart is hardly frequent during class, as most of the younger students are eager to please and flaunt their acquired knowledge to the teacher for the praise they receive— especially since Ms. Birgit is a wonderful teacher who's very supportive and enthusiastic.

Today, like every other day, played out just like that... though mundane, perhaps I'll share with you a shortened version of it.

Ms. Birgit: "How long has Gatsbahlburg existed?"

Younger student: "8,000 years!"

Ms. Birgit: "Hmm. No, that's not correct. Anyone else?"

Younger student: "For forever!"

Ms. Birgit: "That's the one! Now, you were close earlier and already knew the right answer for this question, so why don't you give it to me again— For how long has Gatsbahlburg been *occupied* by us residents?"

Younger Student: "8,000 years!"

Ms. Birgit: "Now you're correct! Okay, let's do some harder questions, shall we! When was the Council formed and what is its purpose?"

Younger Student: "4,000 years ago— immediately after the Prophecy was delivered!"

Younger Student: "To better maintain our community, history, and customs, in peace and harmony until the Prophecy is fulfilled!"

Ms. Birgit: "Very good! Now, what are the Four Pillars that keep our community standing?"

Younger Student: "The Four Fruits and their blessings!"

Ms. Birgit: "And what is the glue that keeps our community together?"

Younger Student: "The Council, tradition, and the abiding of them both by residents!"

Ms. Birgit: "Wow you guys! You've really put in the work to memorize everything, haven't you? Let's see if I can ask you this then without having to call on any of the older students— Why do we have the Gathering-Pit performances?"

Younger Student: "The Gathering-Pit is where the story of the Prophecy— given to us by our greatest and eldest ancestors —is divided into four acts, and played out by the youth during four separate times of the year. Two performances during Day Breaker, and two performances during Night Wafter."

Ms. Birgit: "You are correct about *what* the Gathering-Pit is for. However, my question is *why* do we have the performances in the first place?"

Younger Student: "To remember the story of the Prophecy!"

Ms. Birgit: "Not exactly. You have all been taught the Prophecy here in school, so why do we have to act it out and risk injury, or even death, during the performances?"

Younger student: "Because it's tradition!"

Ms. Birgit: "Yes… but still, no. Let's call on an older student to help us out."

Older Student: "To honor the tradition. To honor our ancestors. To honor the Prophecy. And to honor the Council."

Ms. Birgit: "Very good. Another older student, please. For what reason do we need to honor these things?"

Older Student: "To remind us of it all, and so we may be better aware of the 'pillars' and the 'glues' grandness, compared to our momentary existence in the whole of Gatsbahlburg. We have no more wood here, besides the four trees that bear the Four Fruits; the houses that already stand; the workshops that already hold; the utensils that are already in use; and the handles of the weapons we use in the performance. We have no more metal besides that which rests in sharpened and pointed edges on the ancient weapons used in the Gathering-Pit. By this single example, we must remember exactly why such resources are now only recycled here. We must remember the damage that such weapons had the capacity to cause. And so, all of it is a reminder. A reminder of the chaos that once existed before the Prophecy was gifted to us, and before the eternal peace was created by the Council. The Gathering-Pit serves as both a risk and a sacrifice, to ensure that we never let these dire reminders fall forgotten."

THE SMALL ICY VILLAGE OF GATSBAHLBURG

Ms. Birgit: "Very good. Now, that makes me want to go back a bit to something previously stated, and question it further— Why are our greatest and eldest ancestors considered as those who gave us the Prophecy, instead of the first residents who stepped foot on Gatsbahlburg 8,000 years ago?"

Older Student" "Because before the Prophecy, and before the Council, the first to arrive here and live on this foundation were no different than the newcomers. Gatsbahlburg is a community, and it is only able to be such by the Council's guiding hand; our following of tradition; our remembrance of history; and our individual part in keeping the pace of life here in this village as it is. It is by being a part of this community that we become residents."

Ms. Birgit: "Very good. Very, very good."

⁂

And that was my day at school. An ordinary day.

It's been like that everyday since I turned eight, from then on, everything just began to repeat.

Once some hours had passed and school was finally finished, my friends and I decided to head to the Grove to hangout.

I mentioned the Grove earlier in the telling of this tale, but I wish you could've seen it with your own eyes and realize just how large the space of broken foundation is that creates the giant crescent lake— filled with broken slabs of ice which we leap onto to have our private talks.

Talla, Lukasz, and myself weren't there for longer than five minutes before Dan showed up.

He smiled and nodded his head when we made eye contact, as he slowly closed the distance on his approach to join us.

His hours at the workshop were scheduled for the mornings, and ended in the afternoon, no different than our hours at school—so he and I always managed to hangout after despite his graduation.

"Hey, how was the workshop?" I asked once he was within speaking distance.

"It was good" answered Dan, "A bit harder today than usual.

Since the Gathering-Pit performances are tomorrow, they have us brewing up all the concoctions of the Fourth Fruit double time. It's insane!

I never knew this much preparation went into the performance, or rather, the preparations for everyone who will be observing it."

Me and Dan continued our chat while heading to the edge of the Grove and hopping onto a floating slab, where we then sat for our conversation while Talla and Lukasz engaged in their own private talk on a separate slab of ice.

"Well, I'd rather take on the stress of work from preparing the spirits for the Gathering-Pit, as opposed to having to perform in them" I said, "How does it feel? To not have to worry anymore about what may happen during the performance or possibly getting injured during them?" I asked.

THE SMALL ICY VILLAGE OF GATSBAHLBURG

Dan smiled and raised his eyebrows with a sigh, "It feels good!

The last time I felt this good, like I'm actually able to just enjoy Gatsbahlburg and the life of living in this village, was before I turned ten and had to participate in the performances myself.

Before graduating school and starting in the workshop, I always feared something bad was going to happen on the days leading up to the performance. And then after the performance— regardless of whether I got hurt, someone else did, or we all managed to make it out fine —I immediately dreaded the next one to come, no matter how far ahead in time it was."

"I feel the same way. I was actually talking to Talla about this earlier today, and how I would get rid of the Gathering-Pit performances if I ever made it onto the Council when I get older" I told Dan.

Dan laughed, "Talla will make it onto the Council before you ever do! She's practically made for it… perfect, actually.

I bet she even argued against your hypothetical efforts— that's how much of a perfect fit she is for it.

She never stops talking about her dream of making it onto the Council when she's older, does she?"

"You're right" I confirmed, "She did fight my proposal for removing the Gathering-Pit performances.

But… it was actually me who brought up the matter."

"Really?" asked Dan, perplexed by the idea of this.

I nodded.

"You're not the type to want such things, Hans" he said with an air of seriousness in this statement.

"I know" I said, as if guiltily confessing, "It was because of this morning… my parents… they admitted to me that I'm a prospect for it.

My dad heard it from my uncle, who's currently on the board.

Apparently they consider those who will hold future seats this early on. Pretty crazy, huh?"

Dan looked bothered by what I said, and almost sad.

"I'm sorry" he said, while gazing off at the glistening waters of the Grove.

I huffed awkwardly and smiled, "Sorry? What are you sorry about?

You act as if I've just been sentenced to leave the village during the mate picking."

Dan then looked at me with his eyebrows stern and said, "And you say *that* as if it would be a bad thing.

But that's what you actually want, isn't it? To be selected when you come of age and leave this village— *that* would be your dream, Hans. And you know it."

My fake smile quickly disappeared as I awkwardly swallowed to collect myself from Dan's swift reading of me, "Is it that obvious?" I asked in a low voice.

Dan shook his head, "No. It's not.

But I'm your best friend, so of course it's obvious to me— well, me and my mom."

"Your mom?" I asked.

"Yeah" Dan looked over his shoulder and then around us to ensure that no other kids were within ears' range, despite us being on our own isolated slab, "You already know that my mom was a newcomer and came to Gatsbahlburg where she met my dad— followed by becoming a resident.

Well… she talks to me about stuff."

"She tells you about her previous home?!" I asked, both shocked and ecstatic, hoping to hear anything about the world outside our village.

But to my disappointment, Dan shook his head.

"Not exactly" he elaborated, "She won't tell me about her previous home or what it was like, but she *will* tell me certain things that I know most of the other parents who were newcomers wouldn't disclose to their children, out of fear of breaking the rules.

I guess you could say my mom walks a fine line, but she has her ways of never crossing it. And I honestly love her for that.

I'd feel utterly trapped here if it wasn't for her."

"What does your mom tell you?" I asked, wishing to both experience and be a part of that freedom which Dan experienced from these taboo conversations with his mother.

"Some pretty interesting stuff, actually.

My mom said that she comes from the same village as Talla's dad.

That none of the rules here seem to have a *true* purpose in protecting and nurturing its people.

That the Council, to her, appears like a very strange attempt by mortals to be like immortal leaders… to be honest, I don't know what she means by that. Must be connected to whatever life was like at her previous village.

But she also says that life here is too simple. That community is good, great even, by way and sense of what it brings and adds to life… but the discovery of the self is still crucial, and must be undertaken and pursued by the *individual* in life… and that Gatsbahlburg prevents just that.

It's funny that I was assigned to Spirit Making, because my mother says if this village didn't have such a thing from the Fourth Fruit here, then more people would be like us" he said, gesturing towards himself and I, as if including me in this reference to him and his mother, "But apparently, because of the warmth felt from the community, the security felt from the Council making all of the major decisions, the contentment felt from daily routine, and the comfort experienced from constant simplicity— all topped off by the joyful buzz that is provided by the spirits — no one here seeks *more*.

No one here wants *more*.

Which makes sense to her as to why no one is focused on the self. Because the first step in satisfying that urge— that yearn for '*more*' —will always start with an exploration inward of the self.

'The discovery of the self allows a better perspective for when in pursuit of the discovery to be found outward'

My mom says that's the whole reason she left her village— to discover. And though she did not expect to find Gatsbahlburg, or its rules, or its lifestyle… she did find love.

And sort of like you and how you hope to leave this village one day when you come of age to search for a mate— my mom hopes the same for me.

And honestly, I hope I'm selected to leave, too."

I took a moment to process everything Dan had just told me. To absorb in all of the information he had just spoken, and soak it into me like the sun's warmth on a freezing day.

Though what Dan told me wasn't much, it was still *everything*.

And I felt the most delicate tremble of adrenaline pulse through me from his words, and an excitement which gripped me from every sentence that left his mouth.

After I finished processing it all, I felt a new tingly sensation which could best be identified as gratitude.

Gratitude that morphed into another insatiable curiosity— one which I couldn't help but ask him about.

"How come you're telling *me* this stuff?" I asked, "You know it's risky and a forbidden conversation we're having... even if your mother does walk the line without crossing over it."

"Because you're one of us. Just like I said earlier" he answered.

Dan must've seen that I was still unaware of what he meant, as he then went on to explain further, "My mom said that the people within Gatsbahlburg are simple, and can best be described as being like one of the Four Fruits.

There's those who are like the First Fruit. They nurture this village and nurture its sense of community. They're happy with their lives here and give exactly that back... they're almost too complacent with their simple existence in this simple village.

There's those who are like the Third Fruit. They either need healing, are hoping to heal, or in the process of healing their internal wounds. Most of these people are the newcomers who've arrived, as they have been forced to completely throwaway all of that who they once were, once experienced, and once lived while in their previous homes, surrounded by their previous people and families.

There's those who are like the Fourth Fruit. Joyful and filled with buzz... but also empty. Lifted spirits are their pursuit, and fun times are their way of life here. However, it doesn't go any deeper than that, it's just life to live for the sake of living— not for the experience, not for the growth, and without any desire to develop or become more.

And then there's us" he said, gesturing between us again, "Those who are like the Second Fruit. We seek that light in the darkness. We hunger for truth itself. We desire to go out and find that which is waiting to be found. In the blanket of night— a night of ignorance, structure, and rules —we hold onto the light within ourselves that beckons for more. For something greater. And with our light— our curiosity, our passionate hunger —we guide ourselves as we traverse that ever stretching veil of night that is as much its people as it is the world, in search of more and in search of other light."

I contemplated this example of the Four Fruits that Dan had just proposed to me, immediately placing people I knew into such categories based on what he said.

It made sense, and I was able to connect a lot of people to at least one of them.

Looking back on it, I remember what a special moment that whole conversation with Dan felt like that day. And I couldn't have been more happy or proud of myself to say, as well as for Dan and his mother thinking so too, that I was one of those like the Second Fruit.

Chapter III

BLOOD DRAWN AT THE GATHERING-PIT

The next morning, I awoke with a heavy heart smothered in dread, along with the sensation of nausea... as today was the Gathering-Pit performance.

Today marked the fourth and last one of the year— the final segment of the Prophecy to be read aloud to the crowd, which is the whole village, while the youth displayed the semi-choreographed performance.

I say "semi" because this ceremony is very unorthodox from our other customs by its execution.

Essentially, what happens is the youth who are to perform this day will don themselves in leather— a strange material that is stiff, tough, and very rigid —instead of the common clothes we usually would wear to keep our bodies warm in the cold.

We are then given a weapon, one of the few assorted pieces that still exist in our village, from an older time when we freely waged war on each other when seen fit.

Once we have all the proper equipment on our being, we youths will then perform in the pit, which is a small space enclosed by the elevated seats that the rest of the village observes us from. The onlookers will drink, chat, watch, and listen to the spectacle, while the highest ranking member of the Council recites a specific section of the Prophecy.

During the Council's reading of the Prophecy, the performers both act and battle— carrying out a handful of specific steps, placements, actions, and charades to be done in accordance to the specific verses and passages being spoken. But for the sections where there is no choreography set in place… we are to battle— to strike metal against metal… or even against leather and flesh, should our weapons manage to break through one's guard.

These are the scariest moments of the Gathering-Pit performance, and what makes me and every other participant dread its forced participation as a whole.

We *must* take the battle serious.

We cannot fake our strikes or blows.

Every swing, thrust, and slash must be with the intention to cut down whoever stands before us. To hesitate, hold back, lighten our attack, or to stall and delay any action being taken before the battle segments are over, is the greatest disrespect to the village, Council, community, its residents, and ourselves… or at least that's what we've always been told.

THE SMALL ICY VILLAGE OF GATSBAHLBURG

Of course, I've never quite understood or believed in this reasoning... but the rest of the village does. And because of that, the consequences are heavy should you dare to not elicit danger during your battle.

What are these consequences, you might ask?

Simple things really, not nearly as bad or as dangerous as the performances themselves if you ask me, but they are condemning in their own right— especially in terms of what makes Gatsbahlburg... Gatsbahlburg.

The punishment for not participating in the Gathering-Pit performance or not following through with any violence during them, is that you will be ostracized after by the whole village, including your own parents, for an indefinite amount of time.

No words, glances, or acknowledgment will be thrown your way. And on top of that, you are likely to be chosen to leave the village by the Council when you come of age to find a mate.

I remember witnessing such a mercy occur at the Gathering-Pit when I was younger— when a participant did not go through with cutting down their friend who received many bloody punctures during battle.

Sure enough, when it was all over, everyone acted as if that boy didn't exist after he failed with following through in the violence of his performance, including myself.

I was young then. Naive and not yet old enough to participate in the Gathering-Pit myself. Therefore, I was unable to understand the fear that the boy must've been going through during his performance— not only a fear of getting injured, but a fear of injuring someone you know and are close with.

For three months, no one spoke a word to the boy or even looked in his direction.

But then, one day, I saw his parents hugging and kissing him outside their home before he left for school— wishing him a good day and smiling and waving as he made his way across the village.

And then, during class on that same day, the teacher called on him multiple times to answer some questions about our history, with an extra big smile and loud praises to his correct responses.

In short time following the reengagement displayed by his parents, the other adults also began to say "Hi" to him with smiles. And in short time following the reengagement displayed by the teacher that day, the other kids, including myself, began to speak with him once more and look in his direction.

As I would find out later when I got older, apparently the Council decides when your ostracization is over, and they do this by having a meeting with the parents of the said child, as well as the teacher, to inform them of this decision. After which, the parents and teacher then reengage the child in a public setting so that everyone else becomes aware of their shunning being over.

However, despite his integration back into the community, it came to no one's surprise that he was still selected to leave the village when he came of age to find a mate, and sent off onto the frozen ocean to find a new home.

…I hate the Gathering-Pit performances. Everything about them.

It doesn't make sense to me, nor do I see its value and purpose as a tradition or as some grand ceremony.

But alas, I am to perform in it today. And after this one, I will only have to endure one more year of it before I'm done for good… just four more times where I must risk injury or life, as well as the same upon my friends and peers.

Once the day neared noon, myself and the other performers gathered in the pit before any of the village or crowds could arrive. When we reached the Gathering-Pit, we were then given the leather apparel to wear, as well as our weapons to battle with.

The leather apparel— which we've only been told was once referred to as 'armor' in ancient times —is small, and acts as a hard shell with strings to tie them down with as we adorn it atop the first layer of clothing we wear which serves as our undergarments.

You'd think we'd be cold wearing only one layer of clothing under these sparse pieces of leather to shield us during battle— especially by how substantially low the temperature is during Night Wafter —but it couldn't be more the opposite.

Myself and the others begin to feel our adrenaline rise as the performance edges closer, and that rush of fear sparks a heat within our bodies that make up for the lack of layers we don't wear during the Gathering-Pit performance.

Once we were all prepared, we were then shown to our assigned placement inside of the pit by the Council, who chose where we'd stand before our choreography, which in turn, revealed who we would be battling during the violent segments.

To my dismay, I found myself placed in a position that meant I would be battling Talla… and my heart sank when I saw that she was given the shortest weapon available for the performance— referred to as a dagger —while I was given one of the best persevered ones… a large and powerful longsword.

Following a common theme between Talla and I, she quickly read the apprehensive look on my face that came when I realized how drastically the situation was not in her favor.

She spoke sweet words of comfort to me in an attempt to lift my mood, while the seats surrounding the pit began to fill up with the residents of our village.

"It's okay, Hans" she said, "We'll both be alright, so just give it your all.

We've done this so many times already, and we've always made it out fine. This one will be no different, and neither will any of our final performances in the future.

Just relax. We're of the oldest here. Our experience keeps us safe— no matter what weapons we may be given."

I just nodded and gave a forced smile to show her I was fine, but I couldn't shake the displeasing premonition that was beginning to grow within my stomach.

In short time, every seat at the Gather-Pit was filled with the residents of Gatsbahlburg, and the once low murmurs they buzzed had now become a gentle roar of chatter and laughter, as the spirit of the Fourth Fruit had taken its effect in bringing about excitement upon the community, all gathered up in one place together.

I swiftly spotted my parents in the crowd, who were smiling with giant grins and enjoying the tradition— like most of the other residents were.

I then spotted Dan immediately after, whose eyes were locked onto mine. He gave me a single nod of reassurance— being the only one in the crowd who truly knew how I felt about these performances, and offering alleviation by displaying that shared awareness with me.

Then, the pulsating hum of the crowd's excitement began to die down as the head Council member took his place at the main staging above the pit, and raised a hand in the air to signal the start of the performance.

As the hushes quickly spread amongst the observers in their seats, the head Council member began his introduction of welcoming everyone there, accompanied by all his other words of grandeur.

During this speech, before the performance started, I took the opportunity to scout out Talla's parents.

It wasn't as easy to spot them as I did my own parents or Dan, but I still managed to find them nonetheless.

Talla's mother, being a Gatsbahlburg native, appeared to be enjoying herself and keenly listening to the head Council's speech.

But Talla's father, on the other hand, just stared at his daughter with a look of distraught... the same exact look I had when I first noticed the difference in our weapons.

Why is it that only those who came here as newcomers can also see such things? It's as if those who are born here simply don't notice these things— or will paint them in a different light of no concern, with no recognition or notice that something may be wrong, or at the very least, seem a little off.

"And now, let us begin!" boomed the head Council member, ending my train of thought and trepidation.

Once the performance fell into motion, I was unable to continue a solid flow of thought on the matter of my concerns, as my motor skills took over from the countless years of practice and execution, causing my feet and body to dance and move in the arranged process of the first passage.

"She shall return, and her glowing blue eyes will mark the new age of Gatsbahlburg."

With that first sentence, myself and the others conducted a number of leaps, lunges, and twirls in the air, that could best be described as a beautiful display of synchronized movements. Our breaths could be heard during certain motions, as the exhales and inhales were just as much a vital part of the choreography as the movements were themselves.

I wish I could show you the dance we performed during such segments, as it truly was a spectacle to be seen. If this was what the Gathering-Pit **only** consisted of, then I probably would've been extremely fond of it too, and looked forward to performing it just as much as watching it when I got older.

But alas, the battles were also included in this tradition, and I was quickly taken by a great sensation of loathing, as the next part of the Prophecy was spoken— marking the end of the dance and the beginning of the first battle.

"Only she shall know when, and only she will be the one to choose who will herald us into our next venture, when we ourselves begin to buzz like the bees that we once wished to escape. And with that, her choice will be made, and then will come ours."

While the head Council spoke this passage, Talla and I, who had already locked eyes in preparation, lunged at each other and initiated our clash of metal.

It was to neither of our surprise that I was on the offensive and Talla was on the defensive.

Her short weapon gave her a massive disadvantage to mine, and my aggression was easily staggering and overwhelming during our clash.

However, that's not to say that Talla was an easy fight.

In fact, I did well to not drop my guard, as many moments presented themselves where I was open for a strike to be laid against me, and Talla did not hesitate to seize such opportunities.

Though most of my blows had collided with Talla's blade in the form of parries or guided blocks to deflect the heavy weight of momentum I bore, it was *my* leather armor that was covered in deep and precise slashes from Talla's calculated attacks.

Had we not have such armor to wear during these battles, then Talla surely would've bled me out by now.

But that was not the case, for we *did* wear leather, and this convenient but strange material took all the damage for me instead.

As the head Council neared the final words of the passage, exhaustion and shock from the extreme trembles caused by the parrying and blocking of all my attacks, began to compromise Talla's arm which held her weapon.

And on the final word of that passage, my last horizontal strike blew right through Talla's guard.

Still pumped full of adrenaline and able to react fast, she managed to leap backwards just in time, causing my blade to only cut the surface of her bicep— splitting open the flesh, but luckily not going deep enough to reach the muscle.

Talla instinctually hunched over and grabbed her arm in reaction to the cut, pulling it in tightly towards her chest... however, she had no time to sit with her wound, as the head Council continued his reciting of the Prophecy, and us performers went back to the scripted dance.

"Her choice shall lead us into the new Gatsbahlburg, which is simply the purist state of it which has fled us by our own making."

The second dance was not as graceful as the first, but then again, it never is.

Most are either out of breath from the first battle, which makes their movements sloppy; or are shot full of even more adrenaline, which causes an erratic jitter to replace the elegance of a smooth flow.

For me, it was the adrenaline— one that stemmed from having injured Talla at the end of that previous battle.

And for Talla, who I watched out of the corner of my eye, it was exhaustion.

I knew that we were both battered up from that last battle— since for us, being of the older kids in Gatsbahlburg, our fights were always more dangerous and taxing on the body, whether no injuries be made; whether only the leather is damaged; or whether a true strike lands.

But for some reason, I couldn't shake this unusual feeling that I had... like a very bad hunch... which was only confirmed during my quick glances at Talla from the corner of my eyes while she performed her dance.

"And our choice will be to continue as the residents of Gatsbahlburg... or to find that our evolution and desire of the natural self-transformation has beckoned us back to the center of the pollen."

She undoubtedly was exhausted— more so than the others who also danced out of breath.

This was likely due to the extra exertion and energy it required for her to block and deflect the heavy blows delivered by my much larger weapon— demanding more muscle and strength on her end to be recruited, since her tiny blade forced her arm to take the blunt of the trauma.

On top of that, she was cut... and it was a large one.

I don't know if the dancing caused the wound to split open even more, or if the adrenaline had caused more blood to pump throughout her, and therefore, pour out of the cut... but by the end of the passage and dance, Talla's entire right arm was bright red with blood, as the white under-layer of cloth beneath her leather had soaked up and spread her scarlet life essence with great thirst.

My adrenaline rose higher and my heart sunk deeper, as I realized by this sight of Talla… that she would not be able to fend off such attacks from me anymore.

This last passage to be spoken from the Prophecy… this last battle we would have to endure before the Gathering-Pit performance was over… looked to be like Talla's last if she couldn't hold out for just a little longer to reach its end.

"For with this Prophecy I declare, I tell you all— live; breathe; be; follow your nature and your hearts; grow and flourish by which way you see fit; let it be your own; let it be by only us— good or bad; and let her come again when we ourselves have lost sight of it all and what the outskirts truly entailed, should we ever start to hum— unaware of what such a thing is after successfully being away from it for so long."

During this final passage, I lunged at Talla with a crude and obvious overhead strike.

Though I *did* give it my all and I *didn't* hold back— as per tradition and expectation —I did make sure to have my blows be obvious in their delivery, allowing Talla a slight chance to easily read my moves and react accordingly to keep herself alive until the end.

I had no idea if the residents who observed our battle took notice of this as well, or if they were also aware of how exaggerated my actions were… but surely they couldn't have distinguished my true intentions for them, even if they seemed overtly sluggish, for I continued to put my all behind every slash and thrust, and I can only imagine how animalistic I looked by my brutish attacks.

Talla did well to read them, too, and she didn't fail once in predicating my next strike and blocking it accordingly.

However, that does not change exhaustion. That does not remove injury. And that does not reverse a battered body nearing the end of its defense.

We managed to reach the final few sentences of the Prophecy when Talla's arm finally gave out.

I had delivered another obvious and obnoxious downward strike from above my head, and upon blocking it, Talla lost grip of her weapon and her knees buckled.

Now, she no longer had a weapon… and she was also on the ground.

I felt my body freeze for a moment, and I saw a look of indescribable fear fall upon Talla's face as she looked up at me.

I could also feel the eyes of **every** resident focused in on us, anticipating the unavoidable result of our battle.

But… it was Talla who scooted herself backwards with her leg and her good arm that snapped me out of my frozen state— giving me yet another idea to hold onto the life of my dear friend.

I continued with what I had been doing this entire second battle, and raised my blade high into the air as if to touch the sky, then brought it down with all the force I had. And in response to these obvious strikes, Talla would roll out of the way, leaving me to strike nothing but the sanguine stained snow which she had left behind in her dodges.

Surely everyone knew what I was up to now, but I couldn't care less. And I would've felt utterly alone in my actions too, if it weren't for my awareness that Dan was watching me, and sided with my judgment; Talla's father was watching me, and sided with my judgement; and Talla herself, did not want to die... and for the first time despite her zealous belief in our traditions... I knew that she too, sided with my judgement.

But then...

... Something happened that neither me nor Talla could have predicted.

While avoiding another one of my exaggerated slashes, she ended up bumping her back against the wall that boxed us inside the Gathering-Pit.

Now... there was nowhere left for her to go. Nowhere left for her to roll. No way my telegraphed strikes would aid in her survival any longer.

And with residents being directly above us now, looking straight down onto us from their seats above the wall where I stood over Talla, I had no choice but to raise my sword— unable to fake anything else, anymore.

My last hope for a saving grace, as I lifted the weapon above my head and my elbows past my ears, was that the recital of the Prophecy would end before I could bring my blade back down upon my friend.

"Hoist the totem up tall at the entrance, let us not forget this truth in the centuries that shall pass here."

One more sentence.

Just one more sentence was left to go.

It seemed so simple, and it sounded like no wait at all… but in reality, all eyes were on us, and there was more than enough time that still existed for our battle to finish. A battle in which I was now expected to go through with a killing blow upon Talla.

I could truly feel the eyes of everyone looking at me, and it washed out the comfort I once felt from the eyes of those who watched in favor of my judgment.

I could feel the eyes of my parents. I could feel the eyes of the Council. I could feel the eyes of a younger me, watching like I had all those years ago, when I witnessed that one boy stall before he broke tradition…

And then it came to me— in that last chain of thought.

To *break tradition*, instead of just stalling or hoping for deliverance by the end of the Prophecy's recital!

I realized then that it was *me* who held this blade above Talla— not the eyes who watched us.

It was *me* who held responsibility for taking Talla's life in this moment— not the Council who enforced this tradition.

And I did not want to hurt my friend, nor do I ever want to kill her.

And I do not want to stay in this village, let alone have a seat on its Council when I'm older.

And I did not want to talk to my parents, or any of the residents who live here in Gatsbahlburg, when they are completely fine with this type of madness; completely fine with not asking about the outside world; completely fine with the simpleness and the routine of this village.

I held that sword above my head and gave Talla a smile— a smile that came from the deepest core of my heart, one of true happiness. And I watched as the fear in her eyes immediately vanished at the sight of my smile, and knowing what it meant.

I stood there, still and frozen— like the totem at our village's entrance —just staring at Talla with a smile.

My dear beloved friend was not going to die today.

And more than that— I was to be set *free*!

No more performances. No more talks with my parents. No more expectations. No more enduring this repetition, or the people's contentment who live here. No more possibility of me being on the Council when I'm older. No more wondering or hoping if I will be selected to leave this village when I come of age.

It was all a **guarantee** now— just like my friend's life.

And so I awaited that final sentence to be spoken by the head Council with glee, one which I had never felt so immensely before.

THE SMALL ICY VILLAGE OF GATSBAHLBURG

"And let this Prophecy ring forever until it is closed, and only then may it be forgotten, as the chosen one by her shall write the new one."

… It was over now.

The Gathering-Pit performance was finished.

I released my grip on the sword, which gave a muted clang as it fell onto the snowy ground behind me.

And my smile didn't go anywhere. It only grew bigger as I watched Talla pick herself up, wounded but alive; and as I felt all those eyes of every resident watch in disdain— knowing that I was about to be ostracized and eventually kicked out of this village when I come of age.

I couldn't help but maintain my grin as I looked up, and spanned my vision across the entire seating of the pit which wrapped around me. To see every single resident staring at me, and knowing that I was no longer a part of them or their community. That my deepest internal desire had now been brought forth into fruition!

And it was an even sweeter feeling when my eyes matched with Dan's, and I saw him bearing an identical smile to mine.

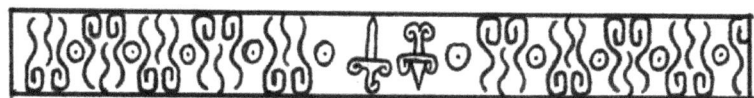

Chapter IV

A PROPHECY FULFILLED

It's strange how immediate it all happened. It felt like there was no time wasted in-between the two events.

To my surprise, though it really shouldn't have been, my ostracization began immediately.

Yesterday— after I dropped my sword at the end of the Gathering-Pit performance —no one said a single word to me… except my uncle.

As everyone left their seats and went back home, myself and the other performers stayed in the pit, awaiting the Council to take back the leather armor and weapons from us.

While untying the straps that kept the leather shells tight against our bodies, I assisted Talla with removing hers, as the wound from our battle made her right arm limp— or at least in too much pain that she couldn't move it in a normal manner.

Talla didn't make eye contact with me once while I helped her. She didn't say a word. Just stared down at the ground in silence, but moved enough in correlation to me undoing her straps that showed me she was accepting my help.

By the time I had finished removing Talla's leather armor and began undoing my own, all the seats surrounding us were empty, and the Council had entered the pit.

All the youth performers then walked to the nearest Council member and handed them their leather and weapon before exiting the pit.

I decided to assist Talla further, as I knew she wouldn't be able to carry all of her leather armor pieces, as well as her weapon, to a Council member.

So while she picked up her dagger with her good arm, I collected all her leather pieces and followed behind her— handing them off to the nearest Council member.

She and a Council member left the pit together, for only a Council member knows and is taught how to use and apply the Third Fruit… and without a doubt… she was in need of it.

Once she left, I went back to our spot where we had fought, and collected my own leather pieces and weapon off the ground to give back to the Council.

When I turned around, however, I noticed that all of them had either left or were making their way out… all besides my uncle, who was the only member that stayed in the pit and watched my approach with a look of anger and disappointment.

I brought forth my items, and he took them from me while not breaking his glare of disdain.

I didn't expect him to say anything, so it caught me off guard when he passed this comment to me in a low and spiteful voice, "I told them we could trust you with this" he said before turning his back and walking out, leaving me to be the last person in the Gathering-Pit… alone— like I figured I would be for awhile now, or at least until I left the village when I came of age.

I guess what took me the most by surprise from this interaction, was that my uncle had actually spoken *any* words to me, despite my supposed ostracization— even if they were words of disproval.

But I guess if anyone was allowed to break that rule, it would be a Council member.

And since I knew by the slip of my parents that my uncle had plans for me to join the Council when I turned older, I guess his anger was enough for him to break such a rule in a single moment of spite.

When I left the Gathering-Pit, not many people were out and about Gatsbahlburg in celebration or drinking spirits, as per usual post performance.

Instead, there were only a handful of people still outside, and they all seemed more perturbed than set in a rampage of festivity.

Most of the residents, had in fact, returned to their homes. And it was one of the quietest post Gathering-Pit celebrations that I had experienced since the last participant broke tradition from when I was a little boy.

I too returned home that day to an even silenter house, and was fed dinner of the First Fruit while neither of my parents looked up at me from their bowls— similar to Talla when I helped her with removing her armor. And similar to my uncle, my parents also bore harsh frowns of disappointment as they stared down at their meals.

I want to say that I went to bed that night feeling hated and shunned... but I honestly can't.

That would be a lie.

For while I laid in bed trying to fall asleep that night, I felt the most at peace than I ever had in years.

Happiness filled my heart with a warmth that not even the adrenaline I experienced earlier that day could ever come near achieving.

And I realized then in that moment, while I was all alone in that dark room, in this tiny village, on this great frozen ocean... that I was smiling again like I had in those final moments of the performance! And just like the glow from the Second Fruit— I felt like a light shining in the dark.

Then, today... the second big thing occurred.

Something which everyone, including myself, would agree is far more grand than my ostracization and what went down prior at the Gathering-Pit.

The early parts of my morning were the same as the previous day.

I awoke naturally for school— my body being conditioned to do so over the years —as opposed to the usual gentle kisses I would've received from my parents waking me up.

I then ate breakfast of the First Fruit without a word spoken between me and my parents, who kept their heads down the entire time.

Afterwards, I put on all my layers to embrace the cold outside and departed home early for school.

I did this for two reasons— to spare Talla and her parents from the awkwardness of my usual knock at their door, since I knew they could no longer interact with me; and to spare my friends from the awkwardness of having to actively not sit next to me in class, or be uncomfortable from me sitting next to them in my usual spot.

Only Ms. Birgit was in the classroom when I arrived that early, and immediately shifted her gaze elsewhere when she saw that it was me who entered.

I then proceeded to take a seat in the farthest corner of the classroom, away from where everyone else would sit, as a courteous gesture to provide my friends with an easier transition into shunning me.

When the classroom started to fill up around the normal time school would begin, I was surprised to see that it was Talla who entered the room last— twisting and turning her head around until she spotted me in the back corner.

She held her eyes on mine with a frown.

I could see an internal struggle conflicting her, and some words budging inside her throat but never making their escape.

When enough of a moment had passed and she still hadn't taken her eyes off mine, nor taken her seat, I too frowned— but in confusion.

To this, Talla finally turned her head from my direction and sat down, causing Ms. Birgit to study Talla in confusion as well, before eventually starting our lessons.

Class went about as usual, and I was not called on once.

I passed most of the time in my own head, as I didn't need to worry about having to answer any of the questions or having to help out any of the younger students.

It was nice, as well as the first time I had actually given any thought to my future, as opposed to just basking in my newfound freedom.

Once school was finished, I was the first one to leave the room since I was closest to the doors, and immediately made my way to the Grove so I could continue my thoughts.

There was still a lot to think about— regardless of how happy I may have been with my decision from yesterday.

Such as the reality that I was never going to experience a warm hug from my parents again. Or the reality that when I *am* selected to leave this village, I will have to trek the frozen ocean to find my new home— a terrifying endeavor, with its reward only lying at the end of such a treacherous journey.

Neither of those ideas weighed too heavy on my conscious, but with no one speaking to me, and in turn, no one for me to speak to— I was left with only my thoughts, and these two things currently filled them.

When I arrived at the Grove, I spotted the perfect frozen slab, already broken and floating outside the foundation's edge. It was further out from the rest and smaller in size, with a generous spacing of water isolating it all the way around.

I made little hops across the split-slabs leading up to it, and then one large leap onto this particular one.

I liked the isolation, and felt proud of myself for providing even more distance for my peers should they come to the Grove at all— no different than how I provided a space between them and myself at school.

However, I was not left to my thoughts for as long as I initially expected to be, as the sounds of Dan's heavy feet crunching over the snow grabbed my attention, and I watched as he took those little hops across the Grove before making the giant leap onto my slab.

His grin now was surprisingly larger than it was yesterday, as he took a seat on the ice directly in front of me.

"So, what should I call you now?" he asked, "Hans the Merciful, or Hans the Defier?"

I exhaled a short and blunt laugh through my nose, "Well, you're defying the rules too right now, so I guess I'll take 'the Merciful' so I can have something of my own."

Dan shrugged and threw his arms up into the air without a care in the world, "As if I was ever bound to this place" he said, "They could select me to stay when I come of age and I would **still** leave here.

There's no way in hell I'm going to abide by their rules and not talk to my friend— especially when I agree with your decision yesterday."

"Huh… I never thought of just leaving even if they did select me to stay" I replied, genuinely awestruck at his thought process.

"It's the same reason for why nobody else in the village is talking to you right now" responded Dan, "Do you really believe that *everyone* wanted you to follow through with the performance and strike Talla down?

I'd bet you at least half of the residents, newcomers *and* natives, were glad you didn't.

But they're still not going to talk to you because they're not supposed to. Because it's a rule. Because it's tradition.

And though they might not agree with it, they **certainly** don't know any other way.

Just like how they forget about the existence of other villages just because they are not allowed to talk about them, so too do they forget that these rules here are not… binding."

"I almost forgot that too, yesterday" I admitted, "In that final moment with Talla.

For a split second… I really thought there was no other choice, and that I was bound to the killing blow because the Prophecy's recital was not yet finished, and the performance was still in motion."

"But you still realized it nonetheless" reassured Dan, "You realized it with enough time— and in the most vital time of when you needed to.

Don't question yourself just because it didn't happen sooner.

It happened. And it happened when it mattered.

That should come as a comfort and a security— not twisted into some flaw of self doubt."

I couldn't help but snort in a happy amazement to Dan's comments, "Maybe Dan the Wise suits you better than 'the Defier'."

"I'll take them both since they're equally true" he responded, boasting a slick smile while confidently leaning back on one arm from his seated position, "Gatsbahlburg has never known the likes of me" he teased.

We both fell into laughter and moved on to a lighter conversation, when a new element demanded both of our attention.

Closing in from afar, and nearing us by crossing the edge of the foundation and into the Grove, was Talla.

She was the only other person to appear at the Grove since school finished— and to our surprise, she too, hopped over the cracks and took a leap onto the slab which we occupied, sitting down beside Dan and in front of me.

"Why didn't you walk with me to school today?" she asked, bluntly.

I felt a little lost for words by Talla's question, and so my response came out choppy and unrefined, "I— I thought you weren't going to talk to me. No one's allowed to. I thought I was being kind by sparing you the interaction."

"Well I'm not going to ignore you, or shun you, or dismiss our friendship" she said with a strength in her voice.

"Talla? Breaking tradition?" said Dan in a mocking manner, equally dumbfounded by this as I was, "What happened to that 'death or tradition' attitude of yours?"

Talla huffed at his words, "When I was met with death *being* tradition— that's what happened. And then I thought: I'd rather be alive and with my friends, than dead for following tradition."

"What about your parents?" I asked.

"My mom's a native. Obviously she's going to follow tradition and probably stop talking to me now for talking to you.

But my dad… he's never held me this much in my life.

There's no doubt in my mind that he's relieved by what you did yesterday, even if he chooses to continue to follow the rules here and not engage you.

But trust me when I tell you, even if his gaze glosses over you, and he treats you like the rest of the residents here— he's the most grateful of them all.

And so am I.

So thank you, Hans."

I didn't know how to respond to her words, as they hit me hard but in the best of ways, so I just smiled and gave her a nod.

"Well, there's no other way for me to put this than bluntly…" said Dan, "But are you sure?" he asked Talla, "I never cared that much for Gatsbahlburg, and I'm sure you're aware of that since you're just as good at reading people as I am.

But Gatsbahlburg has always been a place you've considered home. In fact, I didn't know anyone else who wanted to be on the Council as badly as you did, let alone as qualified, for when they got older.

You're not just gonna be ostracized for speaking to Hans— or me, once everyone finds out I'm still talking to him as well —but you're going to be selected to leave the village when you come of age.

That's permanent, and it's something that *will* happen, even after the Council decides the residents can engage us once more.

Talla… that's as far opposite of your dream as you can go.

But no one has seen you talking with us yet. There's still time to change your mind, or even think about it longer."

Talla shook her head, "Yesterday I almost died.

I never would've made the Council being dead.

And the only reason I'm still alive and it can still be a possibility, is because Hans decided not to follow through with killing me in the name of tradition.

If you ask me… it was never meant to be.

My joining of the Council when I'm older, if followed by the rules of Gatsbahlburg, was fated to never happen, since I should be dead right now by its customs.

And if only my dad and you two are happy about that, then maybe better places lie outside of this village— like where my dad came from.

I'd much rather be alive in a place like that."

Dan patted Talla on the back, "Well then, welcome! We're gonna be hearing only each others' voices for awhile now!"

"I like that" said Talla, "But I don't want to be questioned about whether I'm sure about this decision or need anymore time to think on it again."

She stood up, leaped over the large gap and away from our slab, then began to hop her way across the cracks and back onto the foundation, heading towards where she originally came from.

"Where are you going?" shouted Dan.

"To tell everyone from school that I'm still talking to Hans despite the rules" she replied without looking back at us, "They're all at the Isle right now since they're trying to avoid him. I'd rather let my stance be known now to everyone than wait."

Dan turned his attention back to me, "Huh… maybe I'm not so wise after all. I never imagined Talla would be one to break the rules like that.

… Guess you can't see everything."

Dan and I then returned to our private banter, with the main focus being on his mother and whether she would be willing to inform the both of us on her previous village in secret— seeing has how we were now fated to leave this one.

It had only been ten minutes, maybe fifteen, when our conversation was once again brought to a halt, as Talla could be seen in the distance running frantically towards the Grove in our direction.

Her crazed run was not something that matched with her original detail of simply telling our peers that she was going to remain in contact with me.

It was too erratic— like fear or shock was her source of fuel in this sprint. It resembled the same energy that emerged and carried us through the Gathering-Pit performance.

Dan and I passed a glance to each other in response to this sight of Talla's fast approach, confirming that we both noticed the unusual nature of her sprint, before leaping to our own feet and running towards her to meet her halfway.

When the three of us converged, Talla was unable to get a word out despite our multiple questions and concerns, as she was greatly out of breath from sprinting all the way back from the Isle to the Grove— damn near across the entire foundation of our village!

"Lukasz!" she managed to spit out between gasps for air.

"Lukasz?" questioned Dan, "What about Lukasz?"

"Did he get hurt? Did something happen? Is he okay?" I asked.

Talla shook her head and managed to squeeze out another sentence from her exhausted lungs, "He's in the water."

"He's in the water!?" exclaimed Dan, unable to make sense of what he had just heard.

"Did he fall in? Was he pushed in? Is he out now, at least?" I interrogated further while sharing Dan's confusion.

Talla just shook her head again, but this time, managed to give us a little more insight onto the situation once she was able to muster out a few more words, "The Prophecy! She came!

He's in the water— with *Her*.

The Blue eyes!"

Without missing a beat, Dan and I both grabbed opposite hands of Talla and sprinted in the direction she had just came from, back towards the Isle!

She was completely burnt out from her run to us, but with me and Dan pulling her arms behind us at full speed, Talla merely had to lift her feet without expending any of her own energy, as we made our way across the entire village to where Lukasz and the others were.

Upon our arrival, all of our peers were gathered around a singular spot of the Isle, crowded up and blocking our view.

Dan and I pushed our way through them to the front, never letting go of Talla's hand and bringing her up with us.

When we poked out of the gathered bodies and stood at the edge of the ice where the water began, sure enough, there before our very eyes was Lukasz... and *Her*.

She *was* the Prophecy— the actual physical form of the person, or rather, the *being*, which it spoke of.

Over all these years in which its words were repeatedly beaten and engraved into my head, I never once managed to imagine what this being with Blue eyes from the Prophecy would look like. Or perhaps I just never tried.

But I am certain, however, that in the briefest of moments when my mind did attempt to place a face on the figure mentioned in the ancient literature, that it never came close to what I was witnessing before me now.

The being with Blue eyes did indeed have blue eyes, but they were different from the kind that the residents here in Gatsbahlburg might've bore.

Hers were a bright and brilliant blue, ones which actually glowed in similar fashion to how the ocean would when the sun beamed off its surface.

She looked young, like the age of when we are to find a mate— or perhaps a year or two older.

Her hair was whiter than the snow itself— far different and cleaner than the grey heads of any resident in old age.

Her skin was the gentlest hue of blue— a baby blue... utterly beautiful and delicate.

Though *Her* upper half resembled something of our own bodies, *Her* lower half did not. *She* didn't have any legs, but instead, one large singular piece that began at *Her* hips and stretched down, before tapering and splitting into two small twin-flaps.

This long singular piece of lower body was almost like *Her* legs had been merged together, and it had hundreds of what I could best describe as shimmering fingernails, layered on top of each other. They sparkled with a vibrant green color, far more intense than the green color of the Four Fruit trees' leaves, or the eyes of any resident that flaunted this rare color.

This strange lower body of *Hers* allowed *Her* to float and swim with an unmatched grace in the waters, one which *She* used to dance and parade around Lukasz while he treaded in it beside *Her*.

Lukasz laughed and giggled while spinning in place to keep his eyes on *Her*, as she swam in circles around him while they both bore large smiles— though unlike Lukasz, *She* didn't reveal her teeth with *Hers*, and kept *Her* lips sealed for it.

"Lukasz… what happened?" asked Dan, his voice sounding almost timid from the surrealness of it all.

Lukasz turned his attention away from *Her* and to where we all stood and watched, "Dan! Talla! Hans!

It's the Prophecy! It's actually real! It's happening!

This is it! I'm the one! It's me!"

"How are y— *why* are you in the water?" questioned Dan, further.

"We all came to the Isle after school since we knew Hans would go to the Grove" answered Lukasz as he continued to tread himself afloat in the water, while *She* made laps around him, "Once we were at the Isle, I noticed that the water was moving funny, so I walked to its edge. And once I was standing above the waters, I caught sight of something moving underneath it.

It looked like a shadow at first, but then it grew closer and larger until *She* popped up out of the surface in front of me!

I don't know how to explain it, but I instantly felt a connection to *Her*. I understood immediately who *She* was and what was going on, and so I just… took the plunge into the waters to join her!

It felt right."

"So this is it then…" said Talla, "It's actually happening. The Prophecy is now at play…"

I was taken by my own thoughts during this time and remained quiet, processing what was going on and the madness of it all. But Lukasz must've interpreted my silence as an obedience to my ostracization, as he then spoke directly to me, "It's okay, Hans. You can talk."

I looked up and met with his eyes as he watched me from the water, "Talla's my friend too, and so are you.

I was glad yesterday when you didn't go through with completing the performance. I didn't want her to go, and I didn't want to stop interacting with you either.

But it's okay now— I'm the chosen one!

That means I rule over the Council now. It's my voice over theirs. And I say that you are not to be ostracized for your actions yesterday, and that everyone is allowed to continue to speak and interact with you.

Don't worry, I'll also make sure you aren't forced to leave the village when you come of age.

You shall **not** be punished for sparing Talla's life!" he said with a giant grin, full of pride.

Chapter V

THE ARRIVAL OF MORE EYES

How would I describe the aftermath that followed *Her* arrival, and Lukasz's answering of the Prophecy?

Probably as different… but also still very much the same.

It was now the beginning of Day Breaker— the first long and sunny day of the year.

The lesser ice slabs that surrounded the village's boarders, or floated within the Grove, had begun their slow process of melting and shrinking immensely in size.

School no longer took place— its daily routine had come to a screeching halt.

What purpose was there in telling our history when it was all about to be rewritten? When everything that had been taught was only leading to this moment, here and now, within our village?

THE SMALL ICY VILLAGE OF GATSBAHLBURG

Same went for the Gathering-Pit performances. There was no more worry amongst any of my peers about the next one to come, or the last one to endure before reaching the age of fifteen.

The performances and recital of the Prophecy during it was now redundant… being that the Prophecy was now at play.

We no longer had a need to honor it or remember it— for it was happening in full motion.

Outside of these two changes, however, the normal routine of Gatsbahlburg continued on.

Residents still attended their workshops in the crafting of spirits or candles, for when it came to those two things, *Her* arrival didn't eliminate our need for them. The village still needed to be lit at night, and everyones' mood required a lifting, now more than ever, by the Fourth Fruit's properties.

It wasn't so much that *Her* arrival brought everyone down… just that it made everyone feel a bit lost.

Everything within Gatsbahlburg had been structured into a competent routine— so much so, that every bit of history, tradition, or telling of the Prophecy, acted as a foundation to the structure of that routine, rather than being viewed purely as a reminder to it all which it actually was.

This little shift caused by *Her* arrival was what sparked the residents into feeling a sense of misplacement, rather than *Her* actual presence.

In fact, only two groups genuinely focused on *Her* and what *Her* arrival meant; the younger kids like myself; and the Council.

The Council were actually the most erratic about it, but they managed to display their panicked confusion in a very stable manner.

Lukasz was now constantly in their company, and for many hours of the day, the Council would occupy the school with just themselves and Lukasz— though Lukasz would frequently leave whatever meetings they were having to go be with *Her* in the water; to eat with his family; or on the rare occasion, to hangout with his friends— as he was still a child like us at the end of the day.

And for us youths who now had an exuberant amount of free time on our hands… all day, in fact, since school was no longer in session… all we did was talk about Lukasz and *Her*.

Some of us would gather at the Grove to do so, but most chose to hang around the Isle since that's where *She* stayed and where Lukasz would go to join *Her* in the waters whenever he took a break from speaking with the Council.

Myself, Dan, and Talla were of the few who always went to the Grove to hold our private conversations on the matter.

Dan had even stopped doing his hours at the workshop to talk with us all day.

The arrival of *Her* made him truly have no more investment in Gatsbahlburg.

… Perhaps he knew better than we all did on how deeply things were never going to be the same.

"My mom" said Dan, starting the conversation once the three of us were sat upon one of the few remaining ice slabs in the Gove, "She's told me about more things related to her home. Things that shed light on… or I guess… actually make this whole thing more confusing."

"Your mom's opened up about her original home?" I asked.

Dan nodded, "Not fully, but yes.

She still doesn't go into that much detail about her previous village, but she does divulge new information that relates to the arrival of *Her*."

"What made your mom finally open up like that?" I pressed further.

"Well, she always stuck to the rules and walked a fine line when talking to me about this sort of stuff. You know about this, Hans. I told you a bit about it awhile back, and how she maneuvered around the rules to give me the little information she could without breaking them.

But since *She* showed up, my mother has started questioning the reality which we are nestled within here— but not nearly as much as my father has.

It was him, really. He's why my mom has opened up more about her past.

Being a native to this village, *Her* arrival has hit him the hardest, and so he decided to have a conversation with my mother in regards to this stuff for the first time.

It turns out... he's always had an off feeling about Gatsbahlburg" Dan raised his shoulders and tipped his head to the side, "A *negative* one towards here.

He never brought it up to my mother or discussed it with her, though.

One part because that sort of thing goes against Gatsbahlburg, despite it not being a rule.

Another part because he didn't know how she felt about it herself, and didn't want to fill her with dread or a bad opinion about her new home, since she was a newcomer and he loved her.

And the last part being because of me, and not wanting to corrupt my own outlook on this village.

So his opinion on the matter was always hidden behind a mask— a fake smile and a fake happiness that he would put on everyday.

But once he spoke to my mother about it, she finally became aware of how he truly felt. And with that knowledge, she felt comfortable enough to tell him how she truly felt about it, as well as how I felt.

So, it would seem that my family and I are all on the same page about this place" he chuckled, "What are the odds of that?

Anyway, the only reason my mom didn't divulge more about her village to me in the past, was because of her love for my dad.

She didn't want to break a rule like that, or do such a secretive thing behind his back, because it seemed like a betrayal to the person she loved— and she would never do something of the sort for the sake of that very love.

But now that she knows how he feels and it aligns with hers and my own… well, that line she once never crossed— no longer exists."

"What has she told you now?" asked Talla, with a blazing curiosity behind her eyes, as she was never there during me and Dan's previous conversations about such things.

"A lot" said Dan, with a heavy weight in his voice, "Back in my mom's village, there are five beings that live amongst the residents, and they are like *Her*… they are also *gods*."

"What are gods?" I asked.

"Very powerful beings" answered Dan, "Far different from us residents.

My mom said that the beings in her village and the Blue eyed one that has arrived here are extremely different from each other, but they are gods nonetheless.

The five in her village reign over that land, and she suspects that this Blue eyed being rules over this one.

She admitted that she always found it strange that there were no gods roaming about Gatsbahlburg, since that's the case for her village, *and* every other one that exists on this frozen ocean.

She knows this fact is true for every other village, since hers did not have rules in place like Gatsbahlburg does, and the newcomers that arrived at her home would reveal what life was like from where they came from.

My mom always suspected that the Blue eyed being in the Prophecy must've been a reference to the god of this village, and her theories of such were confirmed when *She* arrived."

"What are the gods like at your mom's village?" asked Talla, "What are the other villages like, and their gods?"

Dan shook his head, "She didn't go into detail. She only spoke of the things that put ours into better perspective."

"What do the gods do?" I asked, "What's their purpose at the villages?"

Dan shrugged, "I asked her the same question. She gave me a vague answer.

They just live here like we do.

Sometimes they protect the village.

But because they are so different— so powerful —we mere residents will never be able to understand their existence or purpose. But it seems they always favor *their* people— those who live on the land they rule."

"What else has she told you" asked Talla.

"That you have a traditional name from the village she and your father are from, Talla.

That she's never heard of a resident being chosen to work hand in hand with the gods who oversee the land, and has no clue what's to come or what will happen next while Lukasz interacts with this Blue eyed being.

That she's nervous, unsure of the future and on what exactly is going to happen now.

That she doesn't remember her way back home on the frozen ocean, and even if she did, there's no way to guide me and my father on the trek out of this place, since it's no longer Night Wafter and the ice has started to melt.

… We are all stuck here— trapped —for whatever the next events are that will play out in this village."

Talla and I looked at each other with discomfort and fear.

Dan was right, his mother's words did make this whole thing more confusing than clear.

It would seem that the only people who had any better understanding on the situation would be Lukasz and the Council, since he had direct contact with *Her*, and the Council shared such contact through him.

"But what about you guys?" asked Dan, "How have things been for the two of you in all this chaos?"

"My parents talk to me as if the events at the Gathering-Pit never happened" I responded, "Same with the whole village, for that matter.

Seems Lukasz kept his word and told the Council I wasn't to be ostracized anymore. And it looks like the Council didn't challenge it, and everyone else has went with it.

Although to be honest... its removal didn't make things feel that different.

Before *She* arrived, I expected that I'd only be talking with you two for the rest of my time in the village. And that's how I still feel.

It's not an endearing thought that my parents only speak to me now, or look in my direction, because Lukasz told them it was okay. If *She* hadn't arrived and Lukasz never made that decision, then they currently wouldn't be doing so— they'd still be ignoring my existence.

But if the Prophecy was never fulfilled, I'd still be talking with you two like I am right now.

I don't know. Maybe I should go easy on them and not see it that way— but I can't help the fact that I still feel hurt and betrayed by how quick they were to shun me... their own son."

Dan gave a silent nod in understanding, "And you, Talla?"

"It's all been a giant change for me" she answered, "After the Gather-Pit performance, my whole outlook on everything changed. **Then** I made the decision to break the rules, expecting my life to change even further by talking to you both the next day. **Then** *She* arrived, and the *whole* village changed. And **now** I'm hearing stuff about the other villages that were once forbidden, along with the different gods within them from you, Dan.

Everyday I don't know what to expect or what I might see or hear. It's terrifying, really— but there's a certain ease I feel through it all because I'm with the two of you during it.

Where I would otherwise collapse emotionally or mentally from how overwhelming this insanity is, I feel like I'm able to be pulled through with the support from your guys' presence.

Sort of like on the day *She* arrived, and how you two held my arms and dragged me across the village when I was out of breath. It's like that."

"Speaking of your arm, how's the cut healing?" I asked.

"It's alright" said Talla, while gently rubbing the wounded spot over all the layers it sat under, "The cut was pretty deep, so the Council told me that the Third Fruit would take a bit longer to fully heal it.

The bleeding and pain had stopped once they treated it on the day of… but it's fallen back in its healing process, and still bleeds every now and again.

… It definitely still hurts."

"What? How come?" asked Dan.

"Eh, it's fine, really. I don't want you guys to think it's your fault or anything."

Dan and I looked at each other with frowns, then back at Talla, "What do you mean?" I asked.

"The cut reopened the day *She* arrived, when you two pulled me across the village" she said.

I figured me and Dan must have both made the same face when our stomachs dropped in guilt from this information, as Talla immediately tried to comfort us and sway our feelings from responsibility, "It's fine! Really!" she said, "It's not like you meant to reopen the cut or hurt me— you guys were just being good friends and not leaving me behind.

I'm glad you guys pulled me with you after my legs gave out, it's just gonna take a bit longer to heal now, that's all."

"Can we see it?" I asked, wanting to know how badly we set her arm back.

Talla seemed hesitant at first, but reluctantly went through with removing the first outer layers that covered her arms and torso. Then, once down to the baggy middle layers, she rolled up the sleeves of her right arm to her shoulder— grimacing the entire time —revealing the red-stained under layers beneath.

Dan and I assisted her from there with rolling up the tighter under layers that covered her right arm, ensuring to not let the cloth scrape or drag against her wound.

Once everything on her right arm was rolled up to the shoulder, and her bare arm was exposed, we inspected the damage that still remained of the cut.

… It was bad.

It looked like it had barely healed at all— as if the Third Fruit wasn't ever applied.

"Talla… why didn't you say anything?" asked Dan, his voice strained at the sight of his hurt friend.

Talla shrugged, "I don't know.

Like I said, it was fine after the performance when the Third Fruit was first applied. But with *Her* arrival and all the thoughts I had after, including our discussions like this one we had… it sort of just fell into the back of my mind.

I probably wouldn't have even thought of it again if you two didn't ask me about it just now."

"Talla, it's a bad wound— a deep one, too" I said, "You need to go to the Council and have the Third Fruit reapplied."

"I will, I will. Promise" responded Talla.

Dan laughed into the first words of his sentence, a laugh of skepticism as opposed to genuine humor, "I'm not taking a promise— we're going **now.**

Who knows what's next to come with the Council, Lukasz, *Her*, and the Prophecy, that'll shake up this village more and prolong you from getting that wound treated.

They might come out with a new rule or some new change to Gatsbahlburg that makes even me and Hans forget about your arm. Let's not risk that, yeah?"

Talla sighed, "Fine, but only if we get to go to your house after the Council treats me. I want to see if your mom will tell us more!"

I jumped up in excitement at the idea, "Me too! C'mon Talla, let's go get the cut treated so we can hear more stories about the other villages ourselves!"

Talla quickly picked herself up off the ground, unintentionally using her bad arm to push up the weight of her body as the excitement took over her too, causing a stream of blood to fall out of the wound.

"You guys…" said Dan, still sitting on the ice, "I don't even know if my mom would be willing to tell more, let alone with you guys by my side. I mean, I don't even know how she'll react when she finds out I've been telling you everything that she tells me!"

"It'll be fine!" exclaimed Talla. She swiped the droplet of blood that streamed down her arm off of herself with a hasty brush of her good hand— sending it into the water that surrounded our tiny isolated slab —before rolling back down all the under and middle layers of her clothes over the wound, followed by putting back on her heavy outer layers. "You and Hans can go to your house while the Council treats me, and hopefully get a head start on informing your mother and warming her up to the idea of telling us more when we are all together. I'll come join you guys after as soon as I'm finished!"

"Sounds like a plan!" I said, taking the leaps off our tiny slab and over the large cracks, making it back to the shore of the Grove, with Talla eagerly following behind.

Dan remained seated there on the small slab without following us, as his way of protesting the idea or at least hoping to change our minds, "Guys!" he called out to us as we made our way out the Grove, "Can we at least talk about this a little more? Or allow me some time to think on *how* I want to ask my mom?"

"Think about it as we walk Talla to the Council!" I shouted back to him.

"And then think about it as you and Hans walk to your house while you wait for me!" added Talla.

"Guys? Guys!" continued Dan in his protest.

Talla and I had made it back to the Grove's shore when Dan's pleads now sounded more like screams of fear than negotiation... something that caught me and Talla off guard, as it was too sudden and too visceral to be related to the current context of our conversation, and must've been related to one of danger.

We both swung around to look back at Dan, expecting to see the worse— such as the tiny slab he was on cracking, or possibly in the process of splitting open while he was still on it.

But what we saw instead was unspeakably terrifying... and only grew worse the longer we watched.

Dan was on all fours as a way to stabilize himself and remain grounded, while the waters beneath him raged and bobbed!

This was extremely unusual— in fact... it was unheard of.

The ocean had a natural push and pull to it, of course, especially the world ocean which surrounded Gatsbahlburg. But its waves were always tiny and superficial— something that just made the surface of the water sparkle from the warping beams of sunlight against it. And for the waters within Gatsbahlburg, its calmness was even greater in subtlety.

But the way that those waters rose and fell now was horrific. It was unstable, like how the spirits of the Fourth Fruit would slosh around inside a mug whenever a drunkard fell into a hysteric spell of sudden dance.

All the slabs and separated chunks of ice in the Grove, bobbed and rolled from these great waves and currents, especially the tiny one which Dan held atop of.

The gaps and spaces between these ice chunks began to grow larger and further apart from these restless waters, and Dan helplessly looked to us in defeat as he tried to secure himself from falling into the water, by balancing broadly on his hands and knees.

Talla and I could only watch in a shared horror for what might happen to our friend... but then Dan looked away from us and down into the waters in front of him... as if something greater and more terrifying had caught his attention.

Seconds later, Talla and I also noticed this new element that called Dan's attention away from us... as a large and bright purple glow threw itself on him, while also illuminating its hue around the entire vicinity which surrounded Dan's area.

I had no idea what was going on, nor what Dan was seeing on his end, but I felt equally petrified just by the look on his face— an immediate sharing of emotion that was transferred to me like a circuit— for no person could ever don the face he did... less they were witnessing a scourge we should all be wary of.

Dan was frozen in fear, as he remained staring at that source of the purple glow which illuminated his entire being.

It was Talla, the bravest of us both, who broke that grip of dread which held us all frozen in time, by calling out to Dan and beckoning him to the shore.

"Dan!" she called out, "Dan, get to the shore!"

Dan finally removed his gaze from the purple glow in the waters to look at us, then shouted back, "**EYES!**"

Talla and I remained motionless after hearing this news, as if it helped hide us from this eerie information— this strange fact. For *eyes* meant a *being*, and in the most primal sense of fear towards the unknown, we did not want this unknown being to become aware of our presence as well.

"Eyes! they're eyes!" continued to shout Dan in a panic, "It's a being! It's another being! The Prophecy never spoke of this! What's going on, guys!"

We continued to just stand there, frozen at the shore, watching him in a fear that only grew bigger within us the more he spoke.

"What does it want? It's big! It's really big! Why is it watching me!? It's just staring at me, guys! What do I do!?" he pleaded.

Reality seemed cruel in this moment, for the ice slabs had been broken apart and separated by the giants waves that surged, to the point where there was no way back or path in which Dan could leap his way across to us at the shore.

It seemed hopeless, and me and Talla felt powerless to help our friend... but we could not abandon him. We could not leave him alone or by himself with this mysterious being.

"You're gonna have to paddle!" I shouted to him.

"What?!" wailed back Dan, doubtful towards the idea, but also aware that his options were short.

"Lie on your stomach, don't look down at the being or into the waters, and use your arms to paddle the ice you're on towards us!" instructed Talla, reassuringly.

"No no no!" begged Dan, "I don't want to move! I don't want to put my hands in the water!"

"You have to, Dan!" I encouraged, "It's the only way to make it back! We'll be right here— we're not going anywhere! Just focus on us, only look at us, and come to us!"

It took a couple of moments for Dan to muster up the courage, but eventually, he followed Talla's instructions and did just that.

It was gut wrenching to watch, and I couldn't imagine what it must have felt like for Dan.

His eyes were filled with tears during the entire time— sobbing as though he knew that something could happen at any moment as he paddled his way towards us on his ice slab.

And that purple glow... the glow that radiated off the eyes he spoke of... followed him, too.

They never let up. They never dulled in glow. They remained constantly below him, watching his every move and following his path, until eventually Dan did make it to us back at the Grove's shore... and me and Talla could see the eyes for ourselves.

They were giant... the two largest pair of eyes I had ever seen— easily bigger than a standing adult's body.

And its gaze... a rich yet brilliant purple, a depth of the color I had never seen before. It held mystery, allure, and a bottomless sense of awareness that made me feel empty in its presence— as if it could see everything and anything passed me, within me, through me, and of me.

It was *haunting*.

Talla and I took hold of Dan's hands once he was close enough to the shore, and pulled him onto the stable ice foundation of the village with a feral strength that we summoned to save our friend.

He immediately crawled a dozen more feet away from the Grove's edge once he made it back onto the solid ice— still taken by a primal fear to get out and away from the danger.

But Talla and I, on the other hand, couldn't help but stay at the edge and observe those giant Purple eyes that laid under the water.

"This wasn't mentioned in the Prophecy" whispered Talla to me, as if to prevent this being from hearing us, "Only Blue eyes were. It never spoke of Purple eyes or any other ones."

"… Something's going on" I whispered back, "Something that's bigger than Gatsbahlburg… Something that's bigger than anything we've been told."

Chapter VI

MY LAST BIRTHDAY IN GATSBAHLBURG

More eyes began to pop up within the week that passed, but those Purple eyes were the first of this surprise.

During Talla's visit to the Four Fruit trees, accompanied by a Council member to treat her wound with the Third Fruit, a pair of glowing Red eyes emerged beneath the waters of the village's pond— eerily staring at her.

And when one boy named Gilbert was playing along the Isle with his friends, a glowing pair of Orange eyes emerged at the edge beside him— its glare locked on to his being.

These new eyes were undoubtedly an unsettling chain of events, but they were nowhere near as frightening as when it happened to Dan— for Dan's was the first of this surprise, therefore, it was not an entirely new occurrence when it began to happen to the others. Though startling... it was no longer foreign.

Not to mention that Dan was out in the middle of the Grove when the Purples eyes emerged beneath him. Everyone else who experienced a similar phenomena was still on the main foundation of Gatsbahlburg when the eyes that claimed them sprung from the rim of the ice's edge.

… Dan was always a bit different after it happened…

At first, he didn't speak to anyone for days, and appeared to still be clutched by the fear we had all experienced.

Then, he slowly began to speak again— but only in response to questions thrown his way, as opposed to initiating the conversation himself.

With more time, Dan regained his voice and would start a topic on his own volition.

But one thing he never did since the arrival of those Purple eyes on him… was smile.

Talla seemed to have handled the appearance of the Red eyes on her just fine. In fact, it seemed to have sparked an excitement in her.

Ever since she disconnected from the ideals of Gatsbahlburg, Talla was always hungry for new information that she once shielded herself from, and took great pleasure in listening to me or Dan's theories about our village, as well as the stories from Dan's mother about the others.

Those Red eyes that took an interest in Talla were no exception to this, and was met with the same curiosity by her.

Gilbert seemed extra hesitant about the Orange eyes that showed up and casted their glare upon him. He was younger than Dan, myself, Talla, and Lukasz, not to mention he was also someone who **didn't** question Gatsbahlburg and its customs— he just went with the flow of it all, like the majority of residents here.

At least with Lukasz, the arrival of the Blue eyes were a part of the village and its history— by way of the Prophecy.

And at least with Dan and Talla, they had already separated themselves from the beliefs held here, and the rules that were to be strictly abided by.

For Gilbert… those Orange eyes that took interest in him were both an unasked for and an inconvenient dilemma— rattling the structure he was already completely fine with and happy to be a part of.

Three things to note about these three new eyes that appeared in Gatsbahlburg, is that One: they never broke the surface of the water. All that could be seen of them were the eyes themselves, and the radiating glow they produced. No bodies nor their full physical form could be seen or ever presented itself above the water's surface.

Two: the eyes always stayed in the place where they first appeared. The Purple eyes that saw Dan, always remained in the Grove. The Red eyes that saw Talla, always stayed in the pond. And the Orange eyes that saw Gilbert, always rested in the Isle. No different than how *She* always remained in the Isle as well, whether by *Herself* or with Lukasz.

And Three: the eyes would only shift their gaze onto the people they first set them upon… or perhaps in the same case as Lukasz's

THE SMALL ICY VILLAGE OF GATSBAHLBURG

circumstance— the people they *chose*. When any other resident, young or old, approached the edge of the waters to catch a glimpse of these new eyes, they would simply stare blankly and straight up into the sky, paying no mind or notice. But when the initial person they saw approached the edge— *their chosen one* —the eyes would move to watch them, and stare at the person for as long as they were within its vicinity.

Oddly enough, it was the other residents who visited these new eyes the most to observe the strange and mysterious spectacle of their appearance, than my peers who were chosen by them.

Perhaps it was because those who were chosen couldn't just simply observe the eyes without them staring back— possibly igniting a sense of vulnerability by the fact that they were being watched and desired, in some form or fashion, by these beings beneath the water.

I always wondered if it was more of a haunting feeling for them, or an honoring one.

But since time is an indifferent force to any and all of the events which happen within one's life... my birthday eventually came around— even amongst this chaos that clouded our village.

It felt, for a brief moment, like a pause in reality. Like a chance to catch my breath. Like a standing of sanity, and a return to the known of what can be expected in the simplest of ways called a predictable day.

... I wish that day lasted longer, or maybe that I appreciated it more. For unbeknownst to me back then, it was my *last* birthday in Gatsbahlburg. And for the first time in my life, I had felt like a normal resident— for I was content with how complacent the early parts of my day went.

Morning was met with hugs, kisses, and love from my parents.

Breakfast seemed fairly normal, as my parents only spoke about me or in a reference to my new older age. Not a word was spoken about the eyes that had appeared in the village, the fulfilling of the Prophecy, or the unknown future for our village.

Noon was spent with my friends, Dan and Talla, and although I didn't expect Dan to talk much, I noticed he put in the effort to focus his attention on me and my special day, despite his mind obviously being eaten by something else which he chose not to vocalize.

Talla also made sure to make me the focus of our conversations, as she would usually be wrapped up in her theories about the eyes and their possible meanings— especially the Red ones that emerged on her.

Even Lukasz spoke to me, which had become quite the rarity ever since *She* arrived.

Usually, his time would be spent with *Her* or the Council. And although he took breaks to be with his family and friends, I never really was among them, as for me, Talla, and Dan were always in our own world together, dissecting everything that was occurring.

But around evening, one of the kids that always hung out around the Isle approached the three of us. He said that Lukasz had sent him to fetch me and wanted to talk, to which Talla and Dan took a step back, and insisted that I have my privacy with whatever this may have been about.

I followed the boy and he led me to the Isle, then to the exact spot along it where Lukasz and *Her* resided in the water.

Lukasz smiled at me when he noticed our approach, then dismissed the boy with thanks.

Once we were alone, Lukasz spoke the first words… the first words I had heard from him since *She* arrived and he granted my ostracization removed, "Happy birthday, Hans!" he said sincerely, with genuine happiness.

"Thank you" I responded, "I'm surprised you remembered."

He frowned, "Of course I remembered. You're my best friend! It's just been awhile since we talked. You know—" he nodded his head at *Her* as *She* nestled *Her* head into his cheek affectionately, "A lot has happened in our village recently, and continues to happen. Between you and me… it's not gonna stop just yet."

Now I was the one who frowned, "What do you mean?" I asked, "Do you know what's really going on here with those other eyes?"

Lukasz looked at *Her*, sighed, then back to me, "There's a lot of things I know now— from both *Her* and the Council… but mainly from *Her*.

It's not fair for anyone else should I speak on them. And to be honest, they wouldn't really understand.

A lot has changed from the original village that our ancestors founded, and this land which *She* ruled last *She* was here."

"Wait" I said, stopping him from continuing, "*She* speaks to you?"

"Of course!" answered Lukasz with a laugh, "How else would I find out about these things from *Her*?"

I shrugged, "I don't know. I've just never seen *Her* speak, or even open *Her* mouth for that matter. *She* seems to just smile and swim with you or around you all the time.

Not even any of the other kids have said anything about seeing *Her* speak."

"That's because no one has seen *Her* speak, for *She* only speaks to me. And yeah… I haven't told anyone else that *She* does, not even the Council.

I guess you're right to find it surprising, then."

"Not even the Council knows *She* speaks to you?… Then why are you telling me?" I asked.

"Well that's a simple answer— because you're *not* the Council. Because you're *not* the other kids. Because you're *Hans*, and *my friend*, and of all the residents in this village who would suffer an unfair burden by knowing the certain knowledges I now hold… you are not one of them."

I scratched the back of my head, confused by what he had said, "Does that mean there's something you know about me that I don't?" I asked.

Lukasz sighed again, "I wish you could see things the way I do now. It would make such questions and conversation easier.

Listen— I know you, Dan, and Talla are the only three kids in the village who have achieved an even *slight* grasp of what is really going on.

You three are very aware that something grander is at play here... and you're not wrong.

Yet, despite all three of you sharing that awareness, only *you* are currently unburdened from yourself?"

"What's that supposed to mean?" I inquired further.

"Dan is burdened, that much is obvious even to you" began Lukasz, "But Talla is as well, though it stems from a different angle than Dan's.

Though she might be more intrigued and excited by the eyes that have claimed her, this infatuation has become a burden, and restricts her in many ways— for now she cannot see the entire picture because excitement entangles her to incorporate those Red eyes into every theory or plot near the truth that might render itself.

Both of them currently burden themselves... except you, Hans.

You're the only one who is as close as one can get to the truth while still shrouded in the veil of mystery, without having adopted a burden.

Even at the Gathering-Pit performance that long time ago, you held no burden from your truth of disobeying the rules of Gatsbahlburg and originally being ostracized. I may not have realized it then, but I certainly can see it now, even when looking back on it as a mere memory— you smiled, one of relief, when you didn't go through with cutting down Talla.

Listen— there's more to come and there's more that's going to happen. And it shall all occur a lot sooner than you think.

I apologize for the distance that has grown between us from *Her* arrival, and the time that's passed since.

So please, allow me to give you this gift for your birthday— a piece of knowledge that will not burden you: When the time comes, choose what *you know* will not burden you. Not the best one, not the right one, simply the choice that leaves you unburdened— for that is *your* truth."

It's obvious to me now what Lukasz meant back then; what he saw; and how he was able to see it then— because of where I am myself now, telling you this story. But back in those moments when he first told me this, I hadn't the faintest clue as to what any of his words meant. They actually made me feel more lost and confused on the situation as a whole. And for that reason, I did not tell Dan or Talla what Lukasz had told me.

Regardless, the three of us continued to hangout together for the rest of my birthday, until night eventually came around and we went our separate ways, returning to our individual homes.

Once I was back at mine, I received two gifts from my parents.

The first one was a new pair of clothes and outer-layers, more appropriate in size for my body.

I was surprised by this gift, for despite having outgrown my old clothes, it was more common that the newer pairs would be exchanged once one turns fifteen and begins working in a workshop.

I guess the reasoning behind me receiving these clothes early, was because with all of the new events happening in the village, all of the common hallmarks of a future now no longer felt promised or like a guarantee to happen anymore.

… It was a bittersweet feeling to receive those clothes and new layers early…

The second gift I received was by far my favorite, and also a common tradition amongst the children who had a parent that was a Spirit Maker. Usually, this special gift would also happen on the same birthday when one received their new clothes, but for the same reason I was given them early, so too was I given this special gift.

Ma and I exited the house together, leaving Pa behind since only she worked as a Spirit Maker, and then trekked to the workshop across the village.

By now, enough time had passed that all the candles were laid out around the village, gently illuminating the pale snow with an amber-ish orange light that expanded and shrunk from the calm breathing of the flames— all while giving the snow a new personality of color, as a twilight blue filled those empty gaps between the neighboring candle's shine, or the spaces that lied between the light and the creeping pitch-black.

When we reached the workshop, we both picked up a candle from out of the snow and made our way inside, using the small dim flames to guide our way.

I had never been inside the workshop before, and was not expecting the pungent smell of the Fourth Fruit's fermentation which had leeched itself into the wood structure of this place after all the years, to burn my nose the way it did.

Nor did I expect the dry "pulling" sensation that the air of the building did to my skin— like the same leeching process had an urge to settle its unanswered thirst through my body for any moisture.

While our candles only gave us a fraction of visible light to see with, Ma was able to use it to the fullest— having already burned a map of the workshop's interior into her head from all the years of working in it.

I felt near blind in that place, but Ma moved effortlessly through rooms, around the corners, dodging tables, tools, and the strange machinery, every step of the way.

Eventually we made it to where the village stored all of the excess spirits that were crafted during day.

Ma then gave me her candle to hold, while she navigated herself around the nearby vicinity in complete darkness, returning to me with a large mug before opening up the storage barrel's lid and dunking the whole mug inside.

When she lifted it back out, the mug was filled to the brim with spirits, and that pungent smell that originally plagued this building now made sense, as I could connect how the fresh spirit would dry and become strung out with time to create this scent that the workshop smelled like.

THE SMALL ICY VILLAGE OF GATSBAHLBURG

However, the fresh mug of spirits still maintained its naturally sweeter and brighter aroma which I was used to— with an even more fruity scent reminiscent of the raw Fourth Fruit from its freshness.

Ma handed me the mug, causing some of its contents to spill out the brim by how full it was.

"It's okay" she said, "This is the Spirit Making Workshop. We spill all the time— it's a part of working here.

If the candles were brighter or the sunlight was out, you'd see how the wood floors beneath our feet are stained rose and plum from all the years of spilling.

Now, take a sip."

I had to use both my hands to maintain control and balance of the heavy mug while steadily brining it up to my lips, then took a cautious but giant swig.

Immediately I was struck with the surprising fact that it was warm. Its temperature was something I did not expect, and it caught me the most off guard.

After that, the sensors in my mouth were rushed with the bubbles from the carbonized fermentation, lathering my tastebuds in a sweet flavor that also held a tad bit of bitterness.

The taste was great, and so was its accompanying feeling in the mouth.

"How do you like it?" asked Ma.

I was at a loss for words, and couldn't stop taking miniature sips to allow my mouth to experience that sensation and flavor on repeat.

I looked up at her and smiled, and she didn't need any more of a confirmation than that.

She caressed my cheek with her hand, planted a kiss on my forehead, wished me another happy birthday, then guided us back outside.

When we stepped out onto the snow, I noticed that the cold air did not strike my body intensely as it normally would.

I remarked this to Ma, who told me that this was one of the many gifts that the Fourth Fruit gave.

She then followed it with saying that the next gift was relaxation, and then the lifting of one's mood.

She told me to walk around Gatsbahlburg as I drank— to experience the fullness of our village with the Fourth Fruit, and to gain a new perspective and love for it that every resident shares.

She said a lot was changing, and that this was something I should experience… in case it goes away.

Ma then headed back home and left me to my own doings, and with a very full mug in hand, I began to walk around the village.

I took larger swigs the more I became comfortable with its taste and sensation that the drink created in the mouth, and soon, I fell into a tranquility from the monotony of being familiar with it— entering a state of bliss created by this.

Soon, I could feel the spirits affecting the way my head felt, as well as my body. These were the other gifts of the Fourth Fruit which Ma spoke of, as well as the altered states of personality which I had witnessed the older residents enter whenever they partook of the spirit.

My body began to grow warmer and tingle with a buzz. My head felt lighter while everything around me began to feel a little more distanced— not in a negative way, rather, as weightless.

These sensations would've been overwhelming to me had I not set myself on a little march around the village, which made me feel a bit more in control as I maintained a rhythmic pace.

For some reason, I found myself at the entrance of Gatsbahlburg.

I stood under the giant sign that bore our village's name, with the large totem standing just beside me.

I looked out without going any further, and watched the trillions of tiny glistening ripples that shimmered off the world's ocean in a silver hue that only occurred at night.

Then, I looked up into the empty and bleak sky— blacker than oblivion… which turned out to be a great mistake as it immediately made me feel dizzy and slightly nauseas.

I didn't want to be overcome by these negative sensations and spoil my night, so I quickly returned to my rhythmic marching to steady my mind and body once more.

It worked, to my relief, but with my clearer consciousness adrift, and my body just moving for the sake of moving, I suddenly

found myself at the Grove— realizing that I had made my way to it out of habit.

This realization only struck when the orange and twilight blue snow below me— which I stared at mindlessly as I walked — donned a violet hue, which grew darker and richer in purple color the more I continued forward.

I stopped and looked up, not wanting to get too close to the Grove's edge while in this state and possibly trip into the waters.

But when I did look up... I was struck with a sight I did not expect to see.

Further ahead, and a whole lot closer to the Grove's edge than myself... was Dan.

My vision was not the best at this point, due to how much spirit I had consumed and how little remained in my mug, but without a doubt I could easily recognize Dan's silhouette against that bright purple glow which he stood above.

He was my best friend. I could notice his approach any day just by the sound of the snow crunching beneath his feet— let alone the outline of his body.

"Dan...?" I called out in a perplexed voice.

Dan didn't turn his whole body around in response, but only his head, taking notice of me with the corner of his eye.

"Hey, Hans" he said in a calm but also sad voice, "Oh yeah, your mom's a Spirit Maker. Wouldn't it still be your next birthday though that you'd get the *night's mug*?"

"Yeah, but she did it tonight for this one instead. My parents also gave me my new clothes early, too" I answered, "I think it's because of how fast everything is changing. They must feel like the opportunity might not arise during my next one."

Dan turned his head and gaze back towards the Purple eyes below him in the water, "That makes sense" he said, "They're probably right for doing that. Things are changing."

"… What are you doing out here though, Dan?" I asked, "It's the middle of the night."

I could hear Dan faintly chuckle, but even his laugh held a tinge of sorrow in it, "Your mom must've given you a full mug" he said, "You sound funny— the Fourth Fruit's definitely lifting your spirits right now. Don't worry, your tolerance will go up the more you partake of it."

"Yeah, I'm feeling it right now. I always wondered what it was like growing up while seeing my parents and the other older residents act differently" I replied, "It's strange, more real than I imagined it to feel, but also kinda fun. I just can't look up though, otherwise I'll start to feel sick."

Dan chuckled again, "Yeah, just keep a leveled head and the dizziness shouldn't be able to catch up with you."

"Dan…" I repeated, more serious this time, "What are you doing here?"

Worry for my friend began to settle in my body, especially after what Lukasz had said to me earlier in the day.

Now Dan turned around to face me, and the sorrow I heard in his voice was apparent in his eyes.

"Sorry" he said, "I know how the Fourth Fruit can make us feel. You must be super confused and probably worried right now.

... I didn't expect anyone else to be out here or show up this late— not even you.

But it makes sense with what you said and how your parents did the *night's mug* now instead of on your next birthday.

... I didn't wanna take away from your special day today— or make you concerned about this at any time, really. I feel like you would've protested against it no matter when I brought it up, so I didn't want to burden you with this at all.

Figured I'd just do it tonight when everyone else was asleep in their homes..."

"Burdened with what?" I asked, "What is *this?*"

"I'm unhappy, Hans... been unhappy for a long time now" said Dan, "I was unhappy when we were little kids— way before you even joined me in my thoughts towards this village —back when I felt and *was* all alone in my opinions towards this place.

I was unhappy when I graduated and had to start in a workshop— giving back to this community which I have nothing in common with.

I was unhappy at the idea that I would have to wait until I came of age before I could ever leave this place... or ever find love.

That's what this is all about."

"About being unhappy?" I asked, seeking more clarification so I could better comfort or reassure my friend appropriately.

Dan shook his head, "About *Love*" he answered, "This feeling of unhappiness I'm constantly enshrouded by stems from loneliness. And that loneliness is specifically tied to a yearning for love.

I hope you do not take it personally when I say I am unhappy or feel alone.

You, Talla, and my parents— specifically my mother —are more than there for me and are endearing company… but it's not the same. It cannot provide for that which I seek and have always longed for.

I'm always hearing it from my mother on how she was able to endure the blindness, the ignorance, and the hypocrisy of this village because she had my father. She was, and is, still in love with him. And that love made all of this… illusion… within Gatsbahlburg something that could never weigh her down or corrupt the happiness she held.

I don't have that…

I never did.

And I get it— I'm younger than my mother, and it's something that is usually found in the future.

But the idea of waiting year after year until I come of age just to be able to find someone who I can feel such a love for, or share a happiness with… it hurts.

And once I do come of age, I'll have to trek out of this village and out onto the frozen ocean in hopes that I *can* find another village, and that such a person exists within it.

Then *She* arrived... and my heart ached in a way it hadn't before... as I saw how *She* swam around Lukasz— *Her* eyes fixated on him with a sparkle deeper than the one my own mom has for my dad.

That's what I've always wanted. **That** kind of care. **That** kind of love.

But it was Lukasz who received such a thing...

Please, do not make the mistake of thinking I wished to be the chosen one— I do not, and I'm glad I wasn't the one. I want nothing more than to detach myself from Gatsbahlburg.

But what I *did* want, was someone to look at me the way *She* does at Lukasz. Not any power over this village, but for someone to dance around me with utter joy the way *She* does to him.

Now, however, I'm unsure if I'll even get to leave the village in the pursuit of that love and happiness I've always desired.

There's no telling what's going to happen next, here. And for the same reasons your parents gave you the *night's mug* early, my leave of this village to find love is also no longer a guarantee.

But one thing that is certain— is that my love is not within this village. I know that much.

… I've always been a bit envious of you and Talla's friendship. Something about it feels like it has the potential to blossom into something more in the future. You both have that going for you if you stayed in Gatsbahlburg.

But not me…" Dan returned to facing the glowing Purple eyes, this time, while also taking a couple of steps towards the edge— placing him right at the rim of the ice before the waters of the Grove below, "I was terrified when these Purple eyes first sprung up beneath me" he continued, "I honestly have no words that can be used to describe the fear I initially felt in those moments.

And as haunting as it might've seemed in the beginning… that fear still didn't blind me like it would any of the other residents in this village to the truth.

And the truth is— these Purple eyes chose *me*, Hans. They saw *me* first.

I always imagined that I would have to leave Gatsbahlburg and arrive somewhere else in order to set my eyes upon someone I could love forever. Yet, the identical thought of someone arriving to Gatsbahlburg to set their eyes upon *me* had escaped my mind as a possibility.

But this being, this Purple eyed being… *She* did such.

I've been sneaking off many nights to come look into *Her* eyes and bask in *Her* violet glow. This is not the first time… but it certainly will be the last.

Her eyes— when genuinely appreciated without any fear to interrupt a sincere observation —are the most beautiful I have

ever seen. They hold a wisdom that's securing, an awareness that's relieving, an honesty that's reassuring, and a gleam only for me that's comforting.

There's no other eyes that hold such a spectacular color as *Hers*, which perfectly matches *Her* soul behind them."

"Dan…" I said, extremely concerned by the way my friend was now speaking, for his strange words frightened me on what could possibly be his next actions, "Just step away from the edge, please.

Keep talking, but let's do it somewhere else.

Let's stay up all night walking around the village and talking.

We can even stop at the workshop and both have some spirits while we walk. Or we can talk tomorrow morning if you'd prefer.

Whatever makes you happiest— I'm fine with either.

Just please, come over here— away from the Grove's edge.

Let's keep talking, yeah?"

Dan appeared unfazed by my words, as if he didn't hear them or chose not to listen.

"If these Purple eyes saw *me*, chose *me*, and wishes to share with me an opportunity where love may blossom… then I will put myself on the line to meet *Her* halfway, and I will not run away in fear from something that I've always wanted.

I can see that much.

... We are like the Second Fruit, remember?"

Dan glanced over his shoulder one final time, and smiled at me. Though his eyes still held that sorrow, his smile looked pure and genuine.

"Dan?" I called out to him, now starting a jog in his direction— as I dreaded more than predicated what his next actions might've been.

He looked down at the source of the purple glow in the water, and without any hesitation or a second thought... Dan stepped off the edge of the ice and into the waters.

"DAN!" I broke into a full sprint but quickly came to halt, as the purple glow immediately grew brighter from Dan's entry into the water— followed by flashing shimmers of light which reached a climax and ended in a single giant flash of powerful force, leaving silver sparkles in the air behind with a fading purple glow.

And with that... they were gone... my best friend and those Purple eyes.

The remaining light from their previous presence slowly diminished from the area, and the Grove returned to its usual black abyss without it.

I stood there in the dark, now completely sober of the spirits that once altered my mood, as adrenaline had flushed my system clean by the sight of what had just occurred.

My mind was still not clear, however, for now I was in shock.

I did not know what I had just witnessed.

Was it the death of my friend? Or his freedom?

His delusion? Or his truth?

His new binding? Or his liberation?

His escape? Or his genuine dream of happiness come true?

I could do nothing more than wonder, as it felt like the whole world I once knew was slowly unraveling before me in a new shattered form— piece by piece.

And the hardest part of it all— no different than the shadowed Grove which I stood in —was that I couldn't see where my place was in all of it.

Chapter VII

GOODBYE AND GOOD LUCK, MY DEAR BRAVE FRIENDS

Let me first state that this chapter will not be a long one— so I apologize to those who may have also been startled by Dan's actions, and felt the same emptiness, or a desire for more, or an answer about what occurred that night on my birthday like I did.

I could go into detail about my sleepless night that followed the event; my delivery of the news to Dan's parents; the reactions met by them, Talla, and the rest of the residents when word spread around; or the deeper emotions I experienced, from a feeling that I somehow failed my friend… while also feeling abandoned by his actions.

But that is not the focus of this story. Those little details may suit better elsewhere— perhaps in a tale that puts the people, their emotions, and their internal turmoils at the forefront.

Which is why it is important for us to remember, and for me to remind you, that this story I am retelling you is about how this small icy village got turned on top of its head.

All of the rest, such as those little details, would just be extra… though I cannot help but divulge a little on my own emotions that were experienced— for it is through me and by my own trudge out of that chaos, that I am able to relay you this story now.

I'll admit, however, I am fully aware that my delivery of this tale has had moments where I break from speaking as if the events are currently happening, to reminiscing them as events of the past.

I had thought that my new position in existence, from where I tell you this story, would make it an easy feat in retelling… but I have noticed that it is actually becoming more difficult as time goes on.

So much of me continues to change with every second that passes— even within these mere moments I deliver a sentence.

I wouldn't be surprised if I am a completely different being by the end of this story… or even forget about Gatsbahlburg as whole, like a faint memory of the past. But that is why it is a good thing I tell you this tale— for you shall remember it better than I.

So, I will offer you another apology— this time for the present and previous tenses being mixed up in my telling. I am sure it will only continue, though I will put an effort into not letting it worsen… but I cannot guarantee anything.

With all that being said, allow me to give you a brief summary on what happened after Dan's departure.

It was interesting to observe the slight shift in dynamics which sprung from his leave.

The Council returned almost immediately to their own private meetings, no longer involving Lukasz or sharing them with him. This went on for weeks, and was followed by the Council gathering everyone together in the village, to deliver a decision they had made.

It caught us all by surprise, but most seem interested and almost relieved to this news.

In a time where so much craziness was occurring, and routine was at its most broken, the residents flocked like lost children to the Council— seeking that forgotten comfort they once experienced by letting these men make the major decisions for them.

Even Lukasz left the water to come onto land and listen to this news for himself.

The Council had everyone gather in the school, and they stood on its leveled stage proudly while everyone took their seats, surrounding them to hear what they had to say.

The first part of their speech centered around how they were aware that so much had happened in Gatsbahlburg that the Prophecy, our history, and our ancestors never prepared us for. They spoke on how it was okay to feel confused and unsure at this time, for it was none of our faults for what was happening.

They then went on to provide comfort and reassurance, stating how they have been working with Lukasz in private as he steps into his role as the chosen one of the Prophecy.

After which, they followed it up by speaking sorrowful words of losing a precious and young resident, Dan, and how he will always be remembered by our community.

I distinctly remember scoffing in silence at this, as Dan's disdain for this place was apparent to everyone— especially the Council —even though he only vocalized it with me.

Then… the Council went on to deliver the *real* news. The *decision* they had made for which they gathered us all there to hear.

With silver tongues, they spoke on how the Purple eyes had arrived in Gatsbahlburg with its gaze fixated **only** on Dan. And how only **after** Dan entered the water with them, did the eyes disappear.

They admitted that they had no idea what or who these eyes were, or what their purpose may have been. But they did know that it was not part of their Prophecy; that each new pair of eyes had come as a surprise and as an uncertainty to the village; that the eyes seemed to have chosen a specific resident of their own volition, and only showed interest in that person by their gaze; and now… one of the new eyes had left the village, after their chosen person joined them in the water.

All the residents mumbled and murmured in agreement, however, I personally don't think any of them had a strong belief or theory on what was truly happening— rather, they just found a comfort in something finally making sense to them within all of this uncertainty they had constantly been surrounded by.

When the Council was met with positivity and agreement for their logic, they confidently proceeded to deliver the decision they had made.

They suggested that anyone who had a pair of eyes emerge from the water on them, whose gaze is fixated only on them… should leap

into the waters to join them— including Lukasz, despite him already being with *Her* in the water for the majority of the time anyway.

They wanted to assign a specific day and a specific time when everyone who had eyes fixated on them— which was only Lukasz, Talla, and Gilbert at this point —would jump into the waters.

This proposal was also met positively, with only a few murmurs of uncertainty or disproval.

To this, they further elaborated that their proposal was purely a good thing. That the Blue eyes belonged to *Her*, were a part of the Prophecy, and that everything pertaining to the handing down of power in Gatsbahlburg over to Lukasz was going exactly how it should.

However, these other eyes that were never mentioned remained an uncertainty, but *who* they were interested in and *how* they shall disappear was certain.

They sweetened their words by going as far to say that the new Gatsbahlburg, which would be brought forth by Lukasz, might even have a different and longer Prophecy created for the next generations to come— a Prophecy that will be better understood and contain the information we lacked now... by the current residents who were selected by eyes joining them in the waters.

They suggested that this could have happened to our ancestors as well, but they didn't go into the waters with the extra eyes, therefore, never fully learning or understanding their presence, and never recording their existence or their happening— putting us all in this lost position we found ourselves in now.

They said that we could be different— we could be better than our ancestors, and we could spare the future residents of our village from all this confusion which we endured now, and so desperately want answers for.

To this, approving nods were made by every resident. And without even asking Talla, Gilbert, or Lukasz for their opinion or stance on this matter which solely involved them… the decision moved forward.

When the day arrived for them to join the eyes, Talla, Gilbert, and Lukasz went to their respective parts of Gatsbahlburg where their eyes always awaited them.

Talla went to the center pond that surrounded the Four Fruits, where the Red eyes glowed for her.

Gilbert went to the far end of the Isle, where the Orange eyes glowed for him.

And Lukasz went to the other part of the Isle, where *Her* and *Her* Blue eyes and full physical form always awaited him in the water.

Each one of them stood on the edge of the ice, awaiting the exact hour when the sun hanged highest in the sky, to take that final step forward and fall into the waters with the eyes that chose them.

Residents had gathered around the person they either cared about most to observe their departure, or the person who was claimed by the glowing eyes they were secretly most curious about.

I had visited each of the three before arriving and staying at Talla's location, waiting with her for the time to come.

Lukasz looked indifferent as he waited. Almost emotionless, besides the smiles he would give to *Her* whenever *She* randomly swam up to the edge of the ice, as if eager for him to rejoin *Her* as he usually would. There was also a hint of knowing in his eyes— similar to that hidden wisdom that rested in them the day he spoke to me on my birthday.

Gilbert appeared hesitant and quietly scared. He would constantly look around at the crowd that gathered around him, chat to his parents nearby for reassurance, or occasionally glance down at the Orange eyes that never took their glare off him. I felt bad for Gilbert— he was young and obviously not in the same position as the older kids who also shared the similar fate of making this venture by the Council's order.

And Talla... Talla looked excited. Eager, dare I say. Her curiosity for these things had only grown in a steep incline since that day in the Gathering-Pit, and I remember seeing a flicker in her own eyes when I told her about Dan's departure with the Purple eyes. I personally think she wanted this, but was too different from Dan to just take that leap and leave everything behind.

This order from the Council appeared to be exactly what she wanted— or perhaps needed —to fully cut ties with the village and her parents and friends, in the pursuit of the curiosity that ate at her being.

Eventually, when the sun reached its peak, Talla and the others made their leaps.

She took only a second to look back at me and her parents, bearing a large grin as a farewell, before stepping off the edge of the ice and into the waters with the Red eyes.

I merely smiled back, but inside of me, it felt like I was about to lose another close friend of mine.

Not wanting to spoil her joy in those final moments, I thought these words loudly in my heart and head… and since I didn't have the chance to say them to Dan, I extended them to him as well despite his absence in this moment.

"Goodbye and good luck, my dear brave friends."

A splash sounded at the end of those words in my private thoughts, followed by a growing glow of bright red before reaching a climax of its shine, then resulting in a strong flash seen even in this daylight… before both her and the eyes were gone.

Apparently the same went for Gilbert— when he eventually mustered the courage to follow through and leap into the water, a glow of the Orange eyes also played out, which reached a climax with a giant flash… then they both disappeared.

Lukasz, however, didn't go anywhere. When he jumped into the water, the Blue eyed being merely danced and swam circles around him in ordinary fashion. It would've appeared that there **was** a difference to *Her* and *Her* arrival at the village— a separation of those other eyes' presence from *Her* own, to this place and its people.

Back then, I couldn't tell you how and why, but please, be patient. For it will all be understood at the end, I promise.

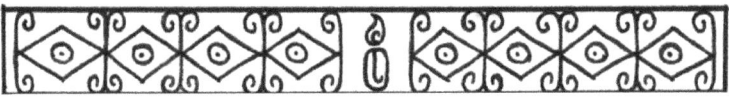

Chapter VIII

THEIR SURPRISING RETURN, AND MYSTERIES UNVEILED

Five days passed. That's all it was.

It seemed short. It *was* short.

No one had time to re-adapt to the old ways of life in Gatsbahlburg we were once so accustomed to before they returned.

And I think that's what we all expected to happen— for the strange business of the mysterious eyes to disappear like the children who left with them, and for everything to go back to normal. That is to say, with the exception of Lukasz and *Her*, of course, who had still yet to bring about any true change to Gatsbahlburg besides the eradication of school and the Gathering-Pit performances.

But such a luxury— as it was considered by most residents — was not to be, and never came to pass.

This happened on the fifth day of their departure, when I was sat near the Grove all by myself.

I was alone for the majority of those five days, as my two best friends had both left, and my relationship with my parents never did return to what it once was before my original ostracization.

Of course, my parents would say different— for they loved me. But my heart never did settle nor feel at ease around them, no matter how much they showered me with affection.

And so, despite their continued company… I felt alone.

And I was alone.

And from a large range of feet away from the Grove, I would sit alone for most of the days that passed.

I never did feel comfortable with being near the waters, let alone atop an ice slab within it, ever since the Purple eyes arrived in that haunting manner with Dan.

So it was by my peripheral vision, as I was drawing in the snow with my finger, that I saw a figure pull itself up out of the water with accompanying splashes.

When I looked up to see the commotion… I saw Dan!

He had returned!

It was a strange sight, for this figure was also a bit different from the Dan I once knew.

He was older, easily over the age to find a mate— but still very much youthful. His appearance was more mature, and his clothes were very different.

But what was most different about Dan, was the way he carried himself. This had been accelerated past any of the other maturities that had altered the structure of his face or body. It could be seen in his expression, and by the way he walked... and as I would soon find out— the way he talked, too.

I sprung to my feet and rushed over to him.

"Dan! Dan!" I called out, almost on the verge of tears from both my excitement and my relief to see my best friend.

He smiled and opened up his arms as we met for a hug. And it was in that embrace that I noticed he even smelt different too, a sweeter scent that was foreign but also comforting.

"Hey, Hans" he said, his voice carrying a slight rumble to it from his new bodily development, while also sounding soft and delicate— as though he was aware of his great change from the last time I saw him... as well as my deep care and unstableness from this moment.

"What happened? Where'd you go? Why'd you leave so fast? How come you've aged so much? Why did you return?" I asked in a bombardment of questions, as tears made a sneaky appearance from my eyes.

"I'll answer your questions, Hans. But first, Talla" he said, with a sternness surrounding that second sentence.

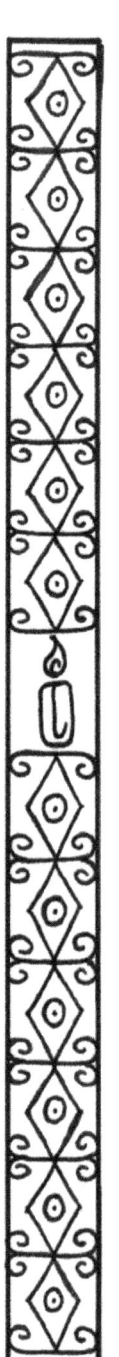

I had no idea what he meant by that last part, but without any hesitation, Dan let go of our hug and made his way towards the pond that bore the Four Fruits with strong and powerful strides— as if he was in a slight rush.

I quickly followed behind him, and upon arriving at the pond, he immediately stood at its edge while giving me a motion to back away from it.

I obliged, and moments later, a red glow appeared beneath to which Dan swiftly stuck his arm out over the waters.

An arm then shot out from its surface, taking a hold of his hand, and Dan powerfully walked back while pulling— allowing this figure he had hold of to effortlessly emerge from the water.

This figure quickly collapsed onto the ice once out, but Dan was able to catch her in time and hold her steady before she could completely fall to her knees.

It was then that I noticed... this figure was Talla.

Similar to Dan, she too had aged some and looked different now. However, her appearance was harder to initially recognize than his. Not because of this new difference in age... but because of how ghastly she looked.

Talla was gaunt; her skin almost grey and devoid of the brown shade and rosy undertones it once held; she was covered in cuts, scrapes, and dried bloody wounds all over her body; her hair was much thinner and more greasy, as if she hadn't bathed; and her demeanor was absent of any joy and energy it once held— replaced now with a timidness and a fear, as her whole body and entire being appeared to be more fragile and far weaker than from before she had left.

I was still a couple of feet back, as per Dan's nonverbal instructions when we first arrived at the pond, but I could hear the words he whispered to our broken friend who he held up on her feet.

"It's okay" he told her, *"You're out of that place now. You're safe... C'mon"* he began to help her walk away from the pond, *"Let's get away from those eyes. You never need to go back."*

I quickly rushed over to help him, placing one of Talla's arms over my shoulder while Dan did the same.

Without speaking, we walked her all the way to her house, where her parents opened the door and quickly took her in.

Dan, who they almost didn't recognize, instructed them to give Talla a bath, change her clothes, and to feed her. He then told them to assist her with all of it, as she needed to regain her strength.

Before leaving them to it, however, his voice changed into something which even rattled my own soul, as he took on a serious tone when he said, "Do **not** ask her about what happened. Do **not** press her to talk. She has just escaped there, she does not need to go back to it in her mind. She will talk... eventually... but leave her be on the topic for now."

They nodded in understanding, or perhaps not understanding, but a recognition of the power in Dan's voice which was not to be crossed.

He then began to walk in the direction of the Isle, and it was during this walk that he answered my questions.

"How long has it been since myself and the others departed?" he asked me.

"Five days" I answered.

"Huh. Well it's been five years for us. Perhaps a bit longer for myself since I left before the others did."

"Five years?... How is that possible?" I asked.

"The eyes— they are all individual beings, just like the Blue eyed one that's with Lukasz. However, unlike *Her*, Gatsbahlburg is not their domain.

Time works differently outside of this place— that is the roughest version I can give you that will allow an understanding for your capacity" said Dan.

"Where did you go? Did you all go to the same place?"

"Me? I went everywhere, but there are still countless places I have yet to see in the scope of infinity" answered Dan, "The others went somewhere else, for those beings with eyes have their own particular domains."

"What does that mean?" I asked, not understanding a single word spoken by Dan.

"All will be answered soon. But this information is important, and must be heard by all the residents in the village as well" he said.

"Okay" I responded, "Um... are you still... *you*?" I asked.

Dan stopped walking and turned to look at me.

His eyes looked into mine, and without being verbal, confirmed my question that it was indeed, him— a single deep look of sincerity that revealed all the most inner parts of him, including the version I once knew.

This was indeed, Dan. He was just a different being now, but still him. And I now understood this.

We continued walking towards the Isle until we reached its edge and waters. We followed it up to the place where Lukasz usually resided with *Her*, however, he was no longer there.

This came to me as a shock, but not to Dan, as he continued walking as if he never intended to stop there.

Eventually we did encounter Lukasz, as he was assisting Gilbert in stepping out from the waters where the Orange eyes lied.

Gilbert was fully out of the water by the time we closed the distance between us, and he too was older, dressed differently, but seemed happier and healthy.

Lukasz turned his attention to Dan after finishing up with assisting Gilbert, as if he knew and expected him.

"Instruct the Council and the village that every resident is to gather in the school" said Dan to Lukasz, "We shall inform them there of what is to come. Myself and the others will explain our individual experiences to the residents, so they may gain a better grasp on the matter. But make the gathering happen at sunset— Talla needs more time to recover."

Lukasz simply nodded.

And with that, Dan turned his back and began to walk away.

※

Before the sun had made its final descent over the world's ocean, the entire village was cramped inside of the school.

Some had seats, some stood in the back, and some sat on the ground.

Everyone was there, and the Council sat in the very front like the astute students would during a lesson, back when school was still in place .

Lukasz, Dan, Talla, and Gilbert, however, sat at the very front of the room on the lifted staging— facing the entire village that had fitted themselves into the building.

Gilbert sat at the far left of the table, then sat Dan, then Talla, leaving Lukasz last at the far right end of it.

I myself stood in the back of the building, standing beside mostly adults, as I had arrived later than the rest of the village since I was informing Talla's parents of our discovery of her, as well as giving details about Dan's appearance.

When a crisp golden color began to pour into the school and fill up the room— a result of the sun's last gleam before hiding away for the night —Lukasz stood up... and the whole room fell silent.

THE SMALL ICY VILLAGE OF GATSBAHLBURG

"Thank you all for gathering here" began Lukasz, "It is crucial that you are aware of the information that is about to be delivered to you— for it concerns all of you, and especially the future of Gatsbahlburg.

I do not want any time wasted or taken away from what is truly important, so please hold your tongues and thoughts— for all of your questions... at least the ones that matter, will be answered by these three, shortly.

One by one, Gilbert, Dan, and Talla will stand and tell you all about what happened when they joined their eyes in the water, and where they went.

This is all connected to something far grander than you may suspect, so it is appropriate that you have some grasp on what is to come, and have some capacity to expect how it will play out.

You may be wondering why these three appear older now, and to quell your minds so you may focus on the more important information at hand, I shall briefly explain it to you.

What was five days to us was five years to them. Dan, being gone the longest, has a few more years on them. These are still the residents you once knew; they are still your children; your friends; your peers; past students; and neighbors. However, they are now more grown— not just of the body, but of the mind and soul too.

I do not ask you to see them as the same person they once were before they left... but I **do** ask you to not see them as foreign— for it is still them, only *more* now.

Please be aware that no question you ask will give you a better filling on what's to come than the words that they are about to say.

Listen. That is the greatest thing you can do now.

Listen, and put everything they tell you together in your own private thoughts. But do **not** get caught up on the unnecessary… there is no time nor room for that.

Gilbert, their ears are yours, now."

Lukasz took his seat while Gilbert rose out of his.

"I left here long ago with the Orange eyed being" started Gilbert, "And the being took me to a world far different from Gatsbahlburg— someplace I could've never imagined or fathomed to exist.

The world I went to had no ice, no snow, and never experienced the harsh bite of cold.

Everything was green, flourishing with plants like the Four Fruits here— expect both bigger and smaller; thinner and thicker; taller and shorter; bearing fruit or no fruit; bearing flowers and different colors… it is safe to say you all know not what I might speak of nor can visualize the full spectrum of it in your minds. But that is okay.

There is an abundance of sustenance there, with fruits that vary in shape, color, texture, and taste, compared to the only Four Fruits here. You can harvest them, grow them, mix them— a beautiful art of creating that which creates food for you to consume, called agriculture, as opposed to only relying on the Four Fruits here which keep stand in their single place.

The nights were just as warm as the day, and when the breeze passed, it did not lash at your face with the fierce sting of frost— rather, with an abundance of sweet and floral scents which the wind had picked up on its journey through the different trees and shrubbery that basks in the same sunlight that nurtures the skin.

The Orange eyes showed me the abundance of life. Life surrounded by life, creating more life, co-creating new life, and existing together in a shared space as such.

I learned a lot there, and grew a lot as well. And I plan to make my return back when the time arrives" Gilbert then sat back down after he finished his piece.

Murmurs were tossed back and fourth in response to Gilbert's speech, and it appeared that Lukasz wanted the people to talk amongst themselves about it, as he remained seated for a handful of minutes while this went on, before standing up again— sending the room into a unified silence.

"Now— Dan" he said.

Dan slowly spanned his gaze over everyone in the entire room, finishing his scoping with direct eye contact on the Council who sat in the front, before standing to speak.

"I…" started Dan, "… Am ashamed. Ashamed of you all— say but a small number here that I can count on one hand with fingers to spare.

You've all failed each other and yourselves.

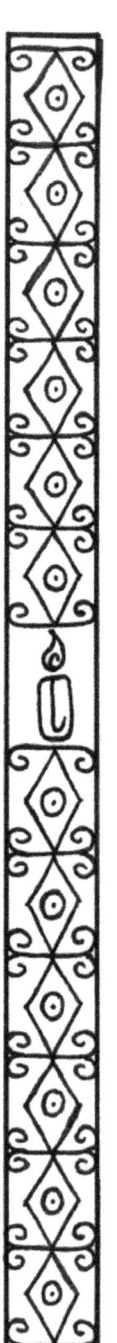

Though you, the residents, still hold a part of the blame... you are not the worst.

That specialty falls only onto the Council."

The Council began to huff at this, some even cutting into Dan's speech and saying how he is meant to tell them of what he saw, not ridicule the village and its residents.

But such rebuttal was not accepted nor allowed to make a full passing, as Dan looked down on the Council— his eyes filled with animosity, and his voice bearing an indescribable power.

"**Silence**" he said to the old men, who immediately obeyed the command, "Now **sit**, and behave like the civilized creatures you claim to be.

I **will** say my piece, you **will** listen, and that **will** be the end of it."

Even I felt my bones quake from Dan's commands. There was no room in them to protest, there was no space left about to argue or reject what he said.

Dan was too far beyond any of us for such a defiance to be possible, and that was very apparent from his presence and his aura.

I think we all felt like children again in that moment— children being scorned by the parent who is far wiser and knew much more behind the wrong that we did than we ourselves were aware of.

"I once pitied you all for being so blind; for being so complacent; for being so naive; for being so willingly ignorant... but now

I shame you for it" Dan continued, "There is so much wrong with this village, and many of you know it.

Yet, not a single one of you has ever stood up against it.

Not one resident has ever voiced it.

Not one soul has ever confronted this place or themselves about the matter.

It was easier to just be a part of the 'community'. It was more fun to just roll with the motion of this village and fall into your place within it— even hoping and waiting at times, for the blessing of ignorant bliss to finally be yours.

You all know what I speak of— you pretend to have forgotten the fear you once felt when the Gathering-Pits were forced upon you. But in truth, you all remember the trembles you experienced from the danger; the dread you felt at the prospect of hurting your friends; the twisting sensations that occurred in your stomachs as the days led up to the performance, and the climax it reached when it finally arrived.

But because you've come of the age where you are no longer forced to step into that pit or continue feeling those awful emotions, you've now thrown all the negativity and awareness of how wrong such a thing was, away— no different than how the dead bodies of Gatsbahlburg are thrown out into the ocean, and forever forgotten.

You do not feel empathy when watching the younger children or newer generations go through that same terrible ritual of fear you all once experienced— not even when it is your own children entering that space of danger.

You are all too caught up in the selfishness of relief; of your own escape from having to participate in it; or in the drinking of spirits and the enjoyment of gathering with the 'community'— as if it is the pit performances themselves that bind you all together.

You throw around the words 'tradition' and 'community' and 'our ways' because you are no longer in the position that once made you question them.

You've let go of all your doubts, fears, curiosity, and hate for such an event the moment you got to put down the weapons on your last performance, permanently.

You then went on to become the same adults who never listened to you, or acknowledged your fear, and forced participation upon you with the threat of ostracization— even when faced with death" Dan huffed a laugh of disappointment, "The Gathering-Pits" he said, shaking his head, "You all once questioned why it was necessary when you were the youths who performed in it, but since you've decided to abandon that question since it is no longer your burden to bare, allow me to re-spark that question.

Why *do* we need the Gathering-Pit performances?

Why does it exist?

What is its purpose?

I can give you the *true* answer to that, for it is not the false answers or dramatic speeches of 'tradition' and 'community' and 'history' which you've all been brainwashed to believe... although, I am unintentionally being kind by proposing the concept of brainwashing, for you all *chose* to fall into the trance-like state of willful ignorance.

The Gathering-Pit performances exist purely to hold power" said Dan, while pointing at the Council, "For *them* to hold onto *their* power.

Fear is used as a tool. A tool to make you obedient.

You all hated and dreaded the Gathering-Pit when you still performed in them, but your parents told you that you must, and that everything was okay— because it was a part of 'tradition'. And your parents before you, told you that because they were told the same by their's. And it goes on and on like that, leading all the way back to the first who were told it— and they... they were told it by the Council.

And now all grown up, you too, tell your own children it when they must participate— continuing this despicable cycle.

You believe that the Gathering-Pits are not a bad thing because you have already served your time in them and survived. So now you spout these empty words, and fall into the delusion that *'The Council really were right!'*. *'The Council* **did** *know what was best, because I did the performance when I was younger, and I came out at the end of it once I no longer had to participate, and I am now happy, drinking the spirit and enjoying myself, since I get to be the observer to the performance rather than the performer!'*.

And so, you obedient fools let go of your original questions.

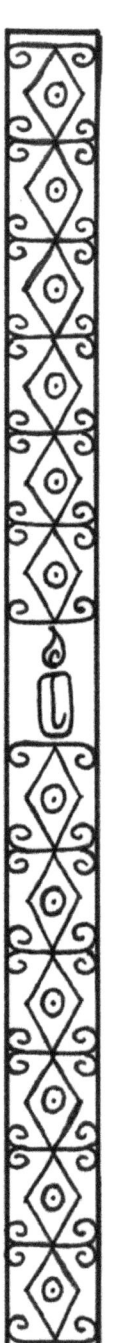

… But you should've kept your questions and your awareness regarding it. For all the danger and the dread and the fear which surrounds the Gathering-Pit, and is felt on the day of the performance, and the whole reason why injuries or fatalities occur… is simply for power.

Not only is this 'tradition' a perfect fear-mongering tool, but it is also the perfect machine to eliminate and maim any potential residents who are best suited to rule, and lead, and guide this village towards true prosperity. The current Council does not want to worry about or risk such residents ever taking hold of a seat on the Council in the future, so they ensure that such residents can never even get the chance. And for those who are not potential threats to the Council, the Gathering-Pit still serves a purpose in ensuring they grow up to be the residents which you are all now, by being tumbled into fear— a fear that keeps you complacent, and them in control.

If the Prophecy never came into fulfillment during our time, and if the Blue eyed being never showed up here and took to Lukasz… then *Talla* would've been the next best hope of a real change being ushered into Gatsbahlburg.

The Council was very aware of this, and in an attempt to eliminate such a potential future from unfolding, they set up the performance to be one that would end her life in death. A dagger for Talla… and a longsword for Hans.

I'm sure when I say this out loud, you are all able to see it now.

But what neither you nor the Council could see, was how Hans' heart was bigger than any 'tradition' held sacred by you oafs.

Look now— at your feet.

Have your eyes opened once more? Do you not see the glistening shimmers of metal shavings which sparkle on the floor?

When the other eyes began to arrive in the village, the Council felt threatened yet again— since it seemed easy enough to them to work with Lukasz in an attempt to hold onto their power... but three more children?" Dan shook his head mockingly as if mimicking the Council in the past, "They stayed up multiple nights in a row, sharpening the weapons of the Pit, and planning a special performance in the hopes that us, who were chosen by eyes, would 'accidentally' kill each other— eliminating the threat against them by our own hands.

It was only by my surprise leave from here with the Purple eyes, that the Council saw an easier solution present itself in getting rid of the other children with eyes.

It's no wonder that they are the only ones who know how to work and dispense the Third Fruit for healing, instead of there being a workshop for it. For how swiftly the fear would fade, if we all had a helping hand when one was injured or to be killed.

But what I speak on now connects to everything— not just the Gathering-Pit.

It connects to the Council choosing who stays and who leaves Gatsbahlburg to find a mate, once the resident comes of age.

It connects to the newcomers not being allowed to speak of their old lives, homes, people, or villages, which they came from.

It connects to how **they** choose who will join the Council, rather than **us**— the residents whose lives they speak for.

It connects to the ostracization that occurs when a rule is broken, and how even parents will abandon their own children to appeal to these ridiculous arrangements that have been structured into place by the Council.

It is not my duty nor my responsibility to hold your hands, and either show or explain all of this to you.

You have souls.

You have the instinct and the intuition to know when something's wrong.

And **you** have the choice to explore it further and question things, or dismiss it and let them be.

It is you and you alone, by your own power, that you choose to do something about it… or do nothing, and forget, and ignore, and be selfish, and just enjoy the life proposed to you in obedience— which is what you have all done.

You already knew. You've always known. And if you didn't, then you chose not to.

I am not chained to be here, to free you, to point out the good and the bad. I have no obligation to any of you or this village.

Unlike the others, I have seen *many* worlds— not just one.

I've expanded my capacity for wisdom, and acquired a vast amount of knowledge to fill it.

My mind and body and soul grew in unison and as one— into the purest form of me —through the travels I made with my being, the one with Purple eyes.

And as such, I grew my own awareness, I gained many perspectives, and I have many eyes myself, now.

It is why I can see so much of the truth… constantly… at all times.

And it is why I can see through everything held here at Gatsbahlburg" Dan took a deep breath in through his nose, calming and recomposing himself while looking over at Lukasz, before continuing his speech, "This place is no longer my concern. The future of this village is in the hands of Lukasz now, which I feel good about. But the future of yourselves is in your own hands.

It is up to you to start asking the questions, speaking up, making the decisions, and letting go of that selfish bliss that is ignorance.

… I honestly can't stand to be here for another moment.

To those of you who I hold dear and give me an ounce of hope for this place and your lives— I bid you farewell, and know that *you* of all people will make the best choice for yourselves in the upcoming future."

Dan then walked around the table, stepped down from the lifted stage, and proceeded down the center of the room— first staring at the Council as he passed them, then meeting his unyielding eyes with any of those who dared to stare at him in anger or spite, though most people in the school kept their heads down in shame.

It felt like a struggle to me when chasing after Dan to follow behind him after he left, as I was forced to push and squeeze my way between the other residents as I rushed after him out the door.

"Dan! Dan! Wait up!" I called out as he stormed across the village, back towards the Grove.

"I'm sorry, Hans" he yelled back, "I know I just came back, but I can't stand to be in this place for another minute.

Hypocrites! They're all willfully blind and ignorant hypocrites.

And the Council— they're the worst of them! Those men are the seeds that leech for more power in the soil, and these residents will till it for them to their delight!

I have to leave this place.

I have no reason to stick around when it's filled with people like that."

I managed to catch up to Dan's heels, but his purposeful and hasty strides kept me just there, "But the village could change with you here" I bargained, in attempt to keep my best friend here with me, "It's obvious to everyone else, just as much as it is to me, that you're beyond different now and can see things in a clearer way than any of us.

The Council wouldn't be able to pull their strings secretively like they have been if you stay. And the people would be forced to see things in a new light from your advice."

"Things are going to change very drastically, very soon, Hans. You just don't know it yet" said Dan, "This village has hope because of Lukasz. If it weren't for him or what's about to happen, then I'd have no hope for Gatsbahlburg.

Only myself and the three others who have been touched by the gazes of eyes are aware of the full spectrum of things to come. Besides the others, it is only you and my parents who bring me any sort of faith, here.

And unfortunately, that is not enough to keep me here for one more moment."

"Well wait… what's this thing that's going to come? What's going to happen soon?" I asked.

"More eyes will arrive, and Gatsbahlburg will change forever" answered Dan, "It's probably best you hear it from Lukasz instead of me, as this domain belongs to the Blue eyed being, and he will explain it best.

But soon, you will all choose which eyes you want to go with— *if* you wish to go."

"But wait. I'm still confused, Dan" I said, a shakiness sounding in my voice as I began to feel overwhelmed by both what Dan was telling me, on top of the sensation of being abandoned by him again, "Why are more eyes coming? How many more? What do you mean we will choose? Does that mean the eyes are going to fall on us like they did you, Lukasz, Talla, and Gilbert?

I want out of here, too. But I'm so lost on how to get out when all of this appears as nothing more than just chaos after chaos unfolding before me, with no real explanation for any of it!"

"Though it is within my awareness, certain things are not within my place to disclose— not even to my closest friend" responded Dan, "... But I will not leave our relationship in such darkness of the unknown. So please, listen closely, Hans.

These eyes that appear— they are gods, as I told you earlier today.

And they are powerful ones at that. Most of them hold a specific domain, or a specific essence, or a specific place within time and space.

When you leap into the water where their gaze glows, you go with them to there— that place they rule, wherever it may be in the universe.

As of now, there are only four eyes here, and they are quite different in their own way from the others that will be arriving soon. These four eyes *chose us* within the village. But the ones to come will choose none, and it is solely up to the resident to go with them— should they choose to leave Gatsbahlburg.

... Be wary though, Hans. Every being is different. None who show up here will hold the same domain, essence, or place. There are as many beautiful and abundant ones as there are cruel and nefarious. Be wise in how you choose, for even a good one does not mean it is right for you."

"... Well then which one should I choose?" I asked, "And your parents, what about for them? Which color do you recommend?

I believe every word you spoke back in the school, so I trust you if you told us which one is best for us to go with— even if it's not perfect for us.

Knowing just a safe one would make me feel a lot better, 'cause I'm still unsure of everything that's going on, and now what's about to come."

Though I couldn't see his face as his strides kept my vision limited to the back of his head, I could sense a hesitation and strain in his eyebrows to my question, but he answered it nonetheless, "We are like the Second Fruit— the flame of the candles.

Tell me, Hans, about the purest flame you've ever seen when staring into the candles that light up this little village at night— they're not yellow, they're not orange, they're not amber… so what color are they?"

It took me a second to think of my answer, before I responded with, "Gold."

He nodded, "The pure. The center.

A return to the buzz, but the most true and untouched start you can have in it all. Go with the Gold eyes if you do not have a calling to any other specific ones, and tell my parents to do the same, please."

A purple glow could be seen ahead, as Dan and I were now nearing the start of the Grove.

I fell silent, realizing that now we had arrived at the place where he would leave… for the second time… and this one felt like it was for good.

But I couldn't help but to continue to follow him, for this was my friend, and I did not wish for him to leave.

His reappearance had brought me an unexpected happiness earlier today, and now it felt like that happiness was being taken away from me— not by my own actions, but by the failures of the others and these residents and Council within the village.

However… I couldn't blame him.

Though I lacked the great insight he had, I honestly didn't require it to understand why he was so disgusted and fed up with this place.

I subconsciously stopped feet away from the Grove's edge as Dan proceeded towards it, watching him from the same exact spot as when I first caught him by surprise at the Grove on my birthday.

As Dan's body became drenched by the purple glow from reaching the ice's edge, he stopped.

"When we first stood here in a similar circumstance, that long long time ago… I remember I told you that I always wanted love, before I took that leap into the water" said Dan, "That's why I first jumped into these waters with the Purple eyes— when it was all still a mystery, and scary, and unknown and unpredictable of what was to happen.

When I joined *Her*, the one with Purple eyes, I received just that— the love I've always wanted… but also so much more.

I never knew that love could and does have so many different forms, strands, and flavors.

I now love myself, the being that I've become, and the awareness I've gained of it all— of everything.

I love *Her* not just for looking at me when *She* first emerged beneath the water when I was atop the ice slab, and not just for choosing me when *She* could've chosen anyone in the village... but for giving me the opportunity to become such a being of who and what I am now.

If there's one thing I've learned, Hans, in all of my time out there with *Her* while exploring the different worlds, universes, and domains— it's that home is not a place, it's a state of being.

Find it in yourself first— don't go and expect it to appear from where the news eyes might take you.

But if a place like Gatsbahlburg prevents you from finding that state of being, then leave here, and go to a new place that provides the proper environment for you to find it" he turned his head and looked at me over his shoulder, "I heard your call... your intention— the day the others left with their eyes.

It was sweet. Genuine and true of heart.

And for that, I would like to wish you the same, and I know you will make the best decision for yourself" he smiled, "Goodbye and good luck, my dear brave friend."

Dan turned his head back around, and looked down at the waters. However, this time, instead of stepping off the edge and into the Grove's water as he did the last time, he simply stood there.

The purple glow then began to grow bright and radiant, and when it reached its peak of illumination, the waters swooshed and moved with a force— similar to the way they bobbed in strong currents when the Purple eyes first arrived.

Then, breaking the water's surface and emerging out of it with the most benign and glorious light ever, was a giant feminine hand.

It was beautiful; pale like the snow; flawless, with the smoothest skin that lacked any imperfections— including wrinkles at the knuckles and joints; and it carried an elegance in its smooth and graceful movements as it cut through space.

The purity and strength of this being's existence was reflected by how the light which radiated out from its skin was almost pure white, with only a tinge of a soft golden glow that was noticed in its hue. And the further the light radiated out, the more its color returned to the purple shade I was more accustomed to seeing from the glow of its eyes in the water.

It looked like time was frozen around it, as its omnipotent presence disturbed the snow on the ground which Dan stood on, but as soon as the snowflakes entered the space of *Her* golden hued white light, they would float in place as if stuck in limbo.

The giant feminine hand then reached out towards Dan, its size easily able to fully encapsulate him with its grip. However, when it wrapped its fingers around Dan to enclose him inside of its hand, it did so in the most caressing and gentle manner, with an obvious love that was readable to any observer on just how much this Purple eyed being cared for him.

With Dan snuggled inside its palm and secured by its delicate grip closed around him, the giant feminine hand then tenderly lifted him off the ground and retracted back into the water… followed by its glow disappearing from the Grove as the two of them immediately left once reunited.

THE SMALL ICY VILLAGE OF GATSBAHLBURG

… I was stunned by that spectacle I had just witnessed.

It was the first time I had ever seen the physical body of a being with eyes that was not the Blue eyed one from the Prophecy.

This one was very unlike the Blue eyed being even though all I saw was its hand, for that giant hand made it apparent that its full body was ginormous.

On top of that, it carried an energy that was so pungent, so strong, so pure and raw, that only now from where I tell you this story do I realize that I was actually exposed to and witnessed the Divine Feminine— a true beholder of it, a Goddess like no other.

After Dan left with the Purple eyed being, I began to make my way back across Gatsbahlburg, to the school where the whole village was still gathered.

I kept replaying the image in my head of the beautiful giant hand that emerged from the water and scooped up Dan. With everything he told me about what was to come and the more eyes that were to arrive, I wondered what type of gods the village would soon find itself surrounded by.

When I finally made it back to the school and entered the building, I was surprised to find the whole place in a furious argument of angry residents pointing fingers at both the Council and each other— as a chaos had ensued from Dan's words after he left them with the truth.

The shouts were an assortment of opinions and stances on the matter, falling onto both sides, and even into areas that were completely separate from the doings related to Gatsbahlburg.

I could focus my ears on any corner of the room, and hear a totally different perspective of where the emotions, but mostly anger, was held around.

Some fury was thrown at the Council in regard to everything they'd done. These residents were clouded with feelings of betrayal or foolery from how strongly they once believed in the traditions and customs, which now seemed like complete lies and a farce.

Some wrath was thrown in defense of the Council and the village's ways, with remarks to how life was fine, normal, and happy until the eyes showed up, and how this feud was all started by a boy who left Gatsbahlburg and returned—proving that the rules like 'newcomers holding their tongues about their pasts' were actually dire in maintaining the peace.

Some disgruntlement by residents was situated in how lost they felt; that this fight about the village was irrelevant compared to what was actually at hand; and the fact that everything was changing not just by the Prophecy being fulfilled, but also from the return of the children who went with the unexpected eyes that arrived.

This heated chatter within the school had been going on since I walked out with Dan, and it continued to go on after I returned… that is, until Talla stood up, resulting in the whole building going silent with their eyes and ears on her.

She didn't look up once when she spoke, instead, her head remained down and her voice remained defeated, but everyone listened closely to what Talla had to say, for we were all curious about what she could've seen or experienced to cause the condition of her current state.

THE SMALL ICY VILLAGE OF GATSBAHLBURG

"Um... it was all red— the place I went to" she started, "Constantly red, from a light source that constantly existed but couldn't be seen. As if the air itself carried the illumination.

And it was all kinds of red; deep red; dark red; light red; soft red; angry red; mysterious red; horrifying red; dreadful red; ugly red; alluring red; lustful red; ... just always red.

And uh... there was no snow, no wood, just metal. Lots of metal.

Everything was made of metal.

I didn't know this, but, uh... metal deteriorates, too— just like the flesh after some time has passed. It turns jagged, and rusted like dried blood. *That* metal was the worst. It would cut into your skin and peel it off if you ever brushed against it or fell onto it" Talla took a deep breath then continued, "I wasn't the only one in that place.

There were many others: other humans, other people, and other creatures of the same nature as us. We would all hide, or run, or sneak, or lie still in the shadows. It was good to find such abandoned spots, especially small tight areas with shadows where you could sleep unseen.

And it was good to meet others like me— same of nature.

Friends were rare, and large numbers were safer. But it was always a gamble putting your trust in others like that... because not everyone was good.

... But there were worse.

That's what we all ran or hid from.

Those other *things* that existed in that domain... they were not of a similar nature to us. They were of a nature akin to that domain— violent, and cruel, and terrible. Full of evil, and hatred, and perversion, and sickness.

I think they might have been from that place, like it was their home, like they were the original residents there— the natives.

They would deliver agony upon us whenever we encountered them, stumble upon them, run into them, or if they found us, or hunted us down.

There was nothing good in that place where the Red eyes took me.

I..." Talla frowned, as though disturbed by her current thoughts, "I still can't tell whether the being with Red eyes merely ruled over that domain and watched the suffering occur below... or if it had a hand in it all— if it extended itself through the native creatures there of a different nature who tormented us, or if perhaps it existed in the very essence of the whole domain, which gave way to the unyielding red that always glowed.

If it's... if it's okay with you all, I don't want to go back there.

I'd like to stay in Gatsbahlburg."

Talla swallowed uncomfortably then sat back down, still never looking up or making eye contact with anyone.

With Talla having finished her piece— which made every resident now filled in about where those who left the village with eyes went —Lukasz stood up.

"Now you have all heard first hand what happened to those who went with the eyes" said Lukasz, "Where they went; what it was like; how their experiences differed; how they changed and grew; and most importantly— the fact that depending on the color of the eyes... they were taken to a very specific place connected to that being who bore them.

This is very important to know, and was very important for you to hear, because over the next two days... more eyes will appear.

Many eyes, in fact."

Gasps, murmurs, and an unsettlement spread amongst the residents in the building.

I, on the other hand, was expecting this news to be delivered, since Dan had revealed it to me earlier. And because of my early awareness, I was able to appreciate and notice things about Lukasz's delivery of this news rather than the news itself.

I recognized a new demeanor in Lukasz— one quite similar to Dan's —that had not been displayed until this moment.

Until now, Lukasz had always acted like he was just along for the ride; or still on the road to figuring things out in regard to answering the Prophecy while working with the Council; or just spending time in the water with the Blue eyed being.

But looking back on it, there were brief moments where he revealed to me more than he was letting on. Such as my birthday and the words he spoke to me. Or when Dan reappeared, and how he already knew what Dan was referring to when he spoke of organizing the village after sunset to 'inform them'.

Not to mention, he was always speaking with the Blue eyed being. And without a doubt, entering the water with *Her* had changed him too— he just didn't go anywhere else like the others did.

For whatever reason, be it known only to him and whatever insight, awareness, or perspective he attained from *Her* arrival... Lukasz hid it all, and played clueless on the matter up until now.

I can only guess why he would do that, but I will not question it, for I'm sure Lukasz always knew what was truly best in terms of how he interacted with the village while having all of this knowledge that spanned far and wide within the village's fate... and how it would all play out.

"On the third day" continued Lukasz, "You will all have a choice: leave Gatsbahlburg by joining one of the many eyes in the water— who will take you to its place, essence, and spot in the universe —or... stay in Gatsbahlburg and remain a resident here, as I and my Blue eyed being usher in a new age for this village.

Things will be different here. Things will be rewritten, and I can personally assure you, this tainted touch that the Council has left behind will be completely purified and removed.

But nevertheless, the choice remains yours.

You are now already aware of what some of the eyes are like, and where they will take you— and those ones will remain here for you to join with, should you choose them on the third day.

The many other eyes that shall arrive here will also be an option for you to pick, though unlike the ones that have already made their appearance, you will not know what they entail.

And for that I say— follow your gut and trust your intuition. Do what makes you happy, and what makes you feel the most at ease.

And should you choose to keep Gatsbahlburg your home, then you needn't do anything on Decision Day than remain on the foundation.

Talk with your family, talk with your neighbors, talk with your friends, and most importantly— talk with yourself.

These next two days might seem hectic, and the third day will feel like… an absolute tragedy for some, and an unfathomable freedom and happiness for others.

Now go home, get rest, and be wise over these next couple days.

But be the wisest on Decision Day."

Chapter IX

GATSBAHLBURG CHANGED FOREVER

This will be another short chapter, as there's not much to say about those three days that passed before Decision Day.

More eyes began to emerge in the waters of Gatsbahlburg, lining themselves up along the edges of the Grove or the Isle. Only one pair of eyes joined the Red ones in the small space of the pond, its glow resting on the opposite side of the waters.

On top of the three eyes that had already become common amongst Gatsbahlburg— Orange with Gilbert, Blue with Lukasz, and Red with Talla —the other colors that arrived in the village were a rich Green, a delicate Pink, a pure and pupil-less Black, a glamorous Gold, a radiant White, a mystique Teal, a royal Crimson, a vibrant Yellow, a soft Violet, and a deep dark Cobalt Blue.

With the arrival of the Gold eyes, I made sure to inform Dan's parents of the news he had shared with me, and how he thought

those ones would be their best bet should they choose to leave Gatsbahlburg.

I personally found the Cobalt Blue eyes peculiar, as they were the only ones that shared the pond's water with the Red eyes, lying on the opposing side of them— across the Four Fruit's little foundation.

From the arrival of all these new eyes, the village had become more alive in the sense that a majority of the residents spent most of their time outside of their houses, walking in groups with their friends or family while observing the eyes and weighing out the different options now proposed to them— possibly trying to get a read on these newer beings and what their essence or possible domain might be like.

For me, only two moments really stood out before Decision Day.

The first one came from a brief conversation I had with Lukasz. He actually spent those two days outside of the waters from his Blue eyed being, allotting all of his time to me and a few other peers of similar age.

When I asked him why he wasn't in the water or visiting *Her*, and if it had to do with a particular element revolving around Decision Day that we weren't aware of, he shook his head and answered honestly.

"No" he said, "There are no more secrets or other withholdings going on.

I'm just aware that I will remain in Gatsbahlburg, as it is my destiny and duty to rebuild and rewrite this village for the life of its current and future residents. However, the same can't be said for my friends, and they might choose to leave with one of the other eyes than stay here.

For this reason, I want to spend these next two days with you and my other friends, for it may very well be the last time I ever get to share a space with all of you again.

It is true that I played a role of false naiveness after *She* first arrived, but that was all related to the same reason I only told you on your birthday that *She* spoke to me, and that the chaos had only just begun— because only you could handle such knowledge without it being a burden.

There's no more need for me to protect this village from the truth, as it has already been laid upon them.

Gilbert, Dan, and Talla did a great job at allowing the residents to fully comprehend what exactly is to entail, as well as the severity in which it will effect them."

"That actually brings me to another question I've had on my mind" I began, "The three eyes that came before all of these others— the Orange, Purple, and Red —why was it those ones?" I asked, "I understand the Blue eyes, for *She* was a part of the Prophesy that's connected to this village. But those three others... I don't understand.

They seem to have some value, or importance, or deeper meaning to Gatsbahlburg by the way they showed up.

And the fact that they came, chose a resident, then brought them back before Decision Day— it's like they had a purpose or

played a role in all of this that's going on in the village, and although extremely minor in comparison, are quite similar to your Blue eyes.

I personally can't make sense of it, but it feels like they were not random— as if they were intricately connected to the bigger plan or orchestration for what was to come next."

Lukasz actually seemed confused by my question, as if it was obvious or like he expected me to have pieced it together myself by now, as he responded with, "Do you not see it?

It was *always* going to be these first four eyes that arrived. Not because of the eyes themselves, but because of *this village*.

It was always this.

This was always a part of Gatsbahlburg— right before our very own eyes, and engraved into the very foundation which supports everything here."

I must admit, it still didn't make sense to me then, and Lukasz's answer didn't shed any more light unto my understanding of the question. Of course it is obvious to me now, but back then, it felt like just another enigma outside of my capacity.

Then, later in the day, came the second most memorable moment before Decision Day… and it was actually a rather sad one.

It happened when me, Lukasz, and Talla were all walking together.

It was the exact night before the big day, and most of the village was outside as well.

THE SMALL ICY VILLAGE OF GATSBAHLBURG

We, like everyone else— and everyone else, like us —were making rounds around Gatsbahlburg, to take in all the eyes and their different colors and presence, since tomorrow would be when we made our choices to go with one or not.

And surprisingly, that night was the most beautiful one I had ever seen in Gatsbahlburg.

It was touched with the amber hues from the candles which lined the normal pathways one would take across the snow at night, but now also bore the bright and foreign colors produced by the multitude of eyes that glowed under the waters.

And for the first time since I've lived here, it felt like an actual community, as everyone was in equal standing and in mutual place, since the upcoming Decision Day was an event in which we were **all** required to participate in, and no one had any leverage over the other in an understanding or a control in this chaos.

If every night in Gatsbahlburg felt like this one, I probably would have never wanted to leave this place, and even would have chosen to stay on that big day.

But alas, this beauty was merely suspended over Gatsbahlburg due to the current circumstances which surrounded it.

This beauty was for tonight and tonight only, and it would be gone when the night was over.

Trust me when I say— the atmosphere, the colors, the ambience, the subtle camaraderie, the *moment*… it was one of those rare times in life where life itself felt the most alive.

Even Talla had begun to blossom out of her shell, and slightly return to her joyful self during this night.

She began to walk with her head up.

She began to chime into our conversations, and even lead them herself at times.

She began to smile again, and joke again, and laugh again. And when I heard that laugh once more, it sounded like the most harmonious song of joy— like a metamorphosis, like an overcoming, and like a return, all at once.

I loved seeing her like this. I loved seeing Talla back to her normal self, but also as *more* now, just like how all the other kids were who left with eyes and came back became more.

The three of us enjoyed our time walking all around Gatsbahlburg together, and at one point, when we were in the midst of a joke and tapering out of it with a shared laugh... Talla stopped dead in her tracks, her laugh ceasing immediately, her smile dropping hopelessly, freezing in place, and becoming utterly motionless like the totem which stood at the village's entrance.

Lukasz and I stopped and turned to see what had captured Talla's spirit, and to this, we noticed her gaze and followed it with our heads. The two of us then realized that we had unintentionally ventured during our mindless walk as we talked... near the pond.

And feet away from us now was a blazing red glow, one which seemed to have sensed Talla's nearby presence, and brightened up as it yearned for her union once again.

Lukasz and I shuffled over to Talla, both concerned for what must've been going through her head right now, or what she must've felt from the sight of that red glow, or what subdued memories might be making a haunting reappearance in her mind.

"*He's* waiting for my return— no —*He's wanting* for me to return" said Talla, keeping her sight steady on the distant red glow.

"He holds no power here, Talla. This is not his domain" said Lukasz, "He will not and cannot get passed me or *Her*. You are just as much safe here as you would be should you leave with any other eyes tomorrow."

"It's okay. *I'm* okay" Talla reassured us, "I too have grown from my departure with the Red eyes. Unlike everyone else with eyes, however, I had to learn to settle into my power after I attained it.

The *gaining* and the *becoming* was not a singular progression that happened in one smooth stroke, instead, it was two separate processes for me.

And although I am still settling into my power and my own essence of the being I have become, I *have* started the process nonetheless, and I've done enough up to this point that I can confidently and safely say— **I AM**, and that being with Red eyes cannot touch me again because **I** say so."

Talla then began to walk away, leaving me and Lukasz as the ones standing around. We quickly scuttled in the snow and caught up to her, continuing on with our night.

Back then, when that whole ordeal happened with Talla and the Red glowing eyes, I remember thinking that everything that

had blossomed within her was going to spoil in that instant when she froze. In fact, the idea of such terrified me, because she was my friend and I loved her, and I hated the idea of her never being the same again.

But the truth is, Talla never would be the same, because like all the others— the three other kids who also left with eyes —she could never be the same after her depart and return. She would forever be *more* after that, and forever eternally is.

Though her process was far more difficult, far more strenuous, and far more horrific than the others' growth, she developed it too, nonetheless. And it speaks titanic volumes about the soul Talla bears, for having been able to stabilize her spirit while in agony to still produce fruit and ultimately prosper while under such circumstances.

Those words she spoke to us on that night are the kind that shake domains, rattle existences, strike fear into the gods and beings alike, and write one's presence onto the fabric of the universe itself.

I know now, truly, from *this* perspective looking back, that Talla's words spoke a thousand lives, and that the simplest deconstruction to the grander message of her words meant: she no longer feared, never would fear, and never needs to fear any other being ever again.

Chapter X

DECISION DAY, THE END, AND FROM WHERE I TELL YOU THIS STORY

Like those first eyes that emerged in the waters of Gatsbahlburg, when everything seemed like a rushing dance of madness… so too have we, dear reader, arrived at the end of my story.

And just like how my peers who went with those eyes eventually returned, so too will you return to your life, and I to my journey, at the end of this tale.

Decision Day was unlike any other.

The sky held still as if it were stuck in a purgatory, and the fuchsia ripples from the sun's early ascent remained permanently in suspension on the horizon.

There was no snowfall, but a constant and easy wind would pick up the flakes already on the ground, and occasionally whistle lightly in one's ear if they perfectly opposed its blow.

THE SMALL ICY VILLAGE OF GATSBAHLBURG

Two sounds could be heard which flooded the entire village: One of them being the splashes created by those residents who had made their decision and followed through with it by joining a pair of eyes in the water. And the second one being the sound of human emotion.

Depending on who you were, where you walked, who you crossed by, ect., would play a great role in what you may have heard that day by the other residents.

The air buzzed from the ceaseless discussions happening at every corner, rim, and edge within Gatsbahlburg. You could hear the humble discussions made by those who thought long and hard, yet still pondered what decision would be best; you could hear the heartbroken bonds being separated, as a lover, child, or friend would leave with a pair of eyes that the others did not wish to go with, and could not chase after them; you could hear the strength in those who felt confident in their decision, and how they used their last words to comfort or reassure their lovers or carers before their leave; and you could hear the fear of regret or the tears of lost nerve, as one who may have already decided on a pair of eyes now doubted their initial judgment, when faced with its glow at the edge of the waters.

It was an assortment of human emotion, a mixture of human choices, a whirlwind of cascading effects... but also a display of independent virtues.

That, along with bits of snowflakes, rode the never ending breeze that flowed throughout the village on this day.

I personally only had one conversation that day— a brief one at that —and it was with my parents during our last breakfast of the First Fruit together.

I think that deep down, they were finally aware of the distance that had developed between us after that day at the Gathering-Pit, for their words were brief but also filled with the typical sounds of when the heartstrings are tugged.

They told me their decision, and how they were going to stay in Gatsbahlburg.

They did not try to interrogate my choice out of me, or try to discover which eyes I might have been thinking about going with. Nor did they try to have me reveal my thinking process on the matter, or try to persuade me to join them on their choice.

But they did, however, state that they were going to be outside on the foundation, gathered around Lukasz and *Her* for the day, instead of remaining inside the house— and should I choose to stay in the village, I could find them there, waiting for me.

They were not alone in this decision, as most of the residents who had decided to stay in Gatsbahlburg had gathered around Lukasz at his spot in the Isle with *Her*, as opposed to just staying indoors.

Most people were either gathered around a pair of eyes having intimate or group discussions, parading around the foundation on their way to the next pair of eyes to investigate or deliberate a choice, or already making the splash into the waters as they took the plunge into their new home.

I myself, could be seen walking alone around the village and observing the different types of groups who went with specific eyes or debated about going with them.

THE SMALL ICY VILLAGE OF GATSBAHLBURG

And I too was no different from any of them, as I weighed and juggled the decision as well.

There were three eyes that appeared to be the most popular amongst the residents of Gatsbahlburg, and interestingly enough, those eyes were of the original four to have arrived.

Many went with the Orange eyed being, as it sounded the most safe, the most pleasant, and the most nurturing, yet still different from this icy land.

Many gathered around Lukasz and *Her* in the Isle, as they either believed in his promise to change Gatsbahlburg and usher in a new and better age of this village… or perhaps because they never could break out of the mold that this place once conditioned them into believing, and staying here was the only option that left them sound of mind and heart.

And surprisingly, many had gathered around the area where the Purple eyed being had once shown up during *Her* first arrival, as well as when *She* returned with Dan… but those eyes were not to be seen anymore.

I had always suspected that Dan and the Purple eyed being were gone for good, especially after his last departure and what he said to me in those final moments before he left… but I would be lying if I didn't admit that, I too, wondered and hoped for them to make a return on Decision Day.

I probably would've went with them if they had been here, and by the looks of the many others who had gathered around their spot and waited in wasteful hope, Dan's words and new state of being had touched their souls too— as something they'd either like to become themselves or even just be around.

One thing I never suspected to happen, however, was witnessing some of the residents go with the Red eyed being after seeing and hearing what Talla had to say.

And yet, I watched a handful of residents depart with that deranged being.

It made me wonder— did they like suffering or want to suffer themselves… or did they just want to see others suffering? Or perhaps they were so fed up with everything at this point, that such a terrible world sounded like a sweet escape to them, as there is no way one could focus on anything else when in the midst of suffering or constantly trying to escape an evil…

Of course, there were those who went with the newest eyes to arrive, and I saw such residents as the bravest of the bunch, since there was nothing fully known about where those domains might have rested, nor what essence they were thrusting themselves into.

As I strode about, observing all these people make their decisions, I began to weigh my own.

I could've just stayed here in the village— join Lukasz and *Her* at the Isle where I knew my parents and Talla also were. By doing so, I wouldn't have had much to worry about. It wouldn't be a gamble like the other choices. Everything would remain the same, remain known as it is now… with just some changes coming in the near future that Lukasz would usher in.

But I didn't like the idea of staying. In fact, I hated it.

It felt like such a choice would be a betrayal to myself at the sole expense of comfort.

Before all of this chaos had ensued by the answering of the Prophecy and the arrival of more eyes... I hated this village. I saw all of its flaws, and later, all of its lies.

Whether this place would turn into a new home, mattered not to me, because it had already left its mark on my being— and *now* was the time to depart from this place which was once responsible for every ounce of negativity that brought my spirit dread.

I did not wish to go with the Orange eyes, as most of the people who once held tightly onto the values here in Gatsbahlburg, were now heading there.

Surely they would not have much room for new growth, if their insufferable mindset was now to be placed in a utopia where things would only get better— reinforcing their way of thought, by no struggle existing to produce a challenge against their previous ways of wrongfully thinking or perceiving the world around them.

There was no chance of me **ever** leaving with the Red eyes, and my mind did not occupy a moment of that for debate.

Though I knew he wasn't going to return, I still clung onto the bittersweet thought of Dan and his Purple eyed being showing up, and how all of my issues would immediately disappear, as his presence— and those eyes being an option —would present the answer I was looking for immediately, rather than me having to find it within myself right now.

That desire for Dan and the Purple eyes, had me questioning about going with the Violet eyes that showed up. I wondered— though a different shade of purple —if they possibly held enough similarities to the being that took Dan. Would I find myself on such a similar path as him, though obviously not in the same manner, if I went with those soft Violet eyes?

But then I remembered the deep and dark Cobalt Blue eyes, which shared the pond with the Red eyes on opposing side.

Those Cobalt Blue eyes were the second to arrive of a blue color, as *Her* answering of the Prophecy and claiming of Lukasz marked the first blue ones to appear in the waters.

Though both were blue, surely the Cobalt were of an extremely different essence than *Her's*, since they sat in opposition to the Red ones in the same water— and the Red held nothing good.

If one shade of color could hold that big of a difference, as seen between *Her* and the Cobalt eyes, then the same could be said for the different hue in purple between the soft Violet ones here compared to the deep rich ones that took Dan.

The Gold eyes *seemed* like my possible escape, but they did not *feel* like my sweet escape.

Dan's parents had already taken the plunge into its waters early in Decision Day, since they trusted the words of their son which I had passed on to them.

I, however, despite trusting Dan's words, did not view them as an answer.

I viewed them as more a suggestion. And I couldn't shake the feeling nor the displeasure in the idea of *having* to go with a pair of eyes and embracing a being to escape here. Such a thought didn't feel whole to me, or like it was completely my own.

It made me think of my original plot to leave Gatsbahlburg, and how it would've been by me leaving this village when I came of age— from the prospect that I would have been selected to leave Gatsbahlburg to find a mate.

It would have been by my own journey across the frozen ocean— a frightful but freeing trek —that would produce to me my new home. A liberating endeavor where the destination may have been unknown, but the outcome certainly was.

That always felt right by my heart. *That* never bore any weight on my mind. *That* was a choice that felt purely like my own, with no interference made by any outside being. One which I could live peacefully with, no matter where I may have ended up.

So, following my gut on the path towards that which made me feel unburdened… my walk slowly drifted in the direction towards the entrance of Gatsbahlburg— the true place of entering or exiting here.

When I reached the arching posts that proudly presented this village's name, I walked under them and past the totem, to the very edge of Gatsbahlburg's foundation, where the ice broke off and an unfrozen ocean swayed endlessly beyond perception.

Standing on that edge, I questioned it all:

Gatsbahlburg; My time here; My life here; My whole existence.

The eyes; The Prophecy; The meaning of it all; The connections between them; The people who I once held dear, and those I could never have imagined life without.

All of the lies; and misunderstandings; and moments of fragility; moments of vulnerability, and honesty.

… So much had been revealed to me, just like so much had been conditioned.

And there was an instance where I wondered if perhaps a pair of eyes that had not been seen before or presented itself to the village just yet, would now emerge before me at the edge of its foundation— being the answer I had been looking for that would make all these things, thoughts, and feelings… become simpler.

But as I stared down at the water, hoping for such a miracle… I saw no eyes appear. Only my own reflection on the water's surface.

The sad reflection of me, looking down at the water, hoping to see something, but only seeing my own eyes gazing back.

… And then it hit me. An epiphany, of sorts.

The beautiful actualization from what had been instilled in me from being raised in this village, and having questioned everything within it to now.

The conditioning to 'never enter the water' by the Council's forbidden ruling, and the noticing of my own eyes in them by the reflection which stared back at me.

THE SMALL ICY VILLAGE OF GATSBAHLBURG

All the doubt that had subconsciously poisoned my mind and eventually became a physical part of my being, was met by the ultimate challenge now of breaking that old rule by entering the water to leave with a being.

With everything I've ever felt, everything I've ever thought, everything I've ever done— surely, I too, was my own being. Similar to how Talla spoke of herself the previous night.

And with my Brown eyes looking back at me in my own reflection, I decided to choose *myself*, just like the first four eyes had chosen my peers.

Feeling no more burden towards Decision Day by this sight, as I trusted this answer before me, I stepped off the outer foundation of Gatsbahlburg and splashed into the waters below, slowly sinking into them— and in a sense, into my own embrace —as it was only me now.

I kept my eyes closed at first, focusing only on the internal feelings that stirred from what I had just done.

But slowly, my attention was brought back to the front of my consciousness again.

It was then that I realized that within these waters, I no longer felt the cold in the way which I had become so accustomed to on the village's surface.

I felt a sense of peace, and a calm, and a serenity that I never knew existed within this state of life or physical being.

I opened my eyes, and could see very clearly under the water— immediately taking notice of the beautiful clusters of glowing lights and shimmering sparkles from the stars and galaxies in the far far distance.

Of course, I didn't know it immediately then that that's what they were, but my awareness and understandings of things grew fast and instantly with new wisdom and information the longer I stayed in the water.

I began to swim deeper downwards, heading towards all of those stars and galaxies in the distance, while the water became even warmer and my consciousness expanded even further in capacity the further I went.

I hadn't gotten too far— in fact, I had barely made any distance as I was not fully aware just yet on how far those stars and galaxies were from me —when I heard the faint sounds of splashing in the rear, which made me halt my underwater-swim and turn around to look behind me.

And that is when I saw it— my village from a new perspective.

The underbelly of the giant ice slab which floated as Gatsbahlburg's foundation, as well as all the cracks and gaps in it.

And from the cracks and gaps which made up the Isle, the Grove, and the pond— I saw the splashes of residents who continued to leap into the waters, joining with their eyes of choice.

From underneath that icy foundation… I saw the full physical bodies of the gods who once were just eyes to me, and the spectacle at hand as they teleported the residents so effortlessly into their domain with either a single wave of their hand, or by consuming them into their bellies.

Some of those beings' physical forms were small. Some were gigantic. Some were breathtakingly beautiful. Some were absolutely horrifying. Some had bodies which looked no different than the human form I had been surrounded by my entire life and bore myself. While some had bodies of indescribable features which fell outside of the capacity for the imagination.

And then, as if all those beings sensed *my* eyes on them, they all turned at the same moment in sync to look at me.

For only the briefest of moments, a second of a second of a second… I felt the most world-shattering terror at the sight of them all placing their attention onto me.

An unholy vulnerability to be witnessed by all these different and powerful beings at once— all of these *gods* —while no longer being protected by the surface of Gatsbahlburg, and instead, sharing the same waters which they swam in.

But that fraction of a second where I experienced this terror vanished as quickly as it came, for with my ever expanding consciousness and capacity for understanding, I realized that the fright I felt came from only the small piece of the village that still remained in me.

That small part of me that was still within Gatsbahlburg was swift to flee, though. For I was out of that village now; and I was no longer attached to it; and I was no longer bound to its doings or rules.

And I was no longer attached to any of those beings— the residents —who continued to leap into the water and embrace those gods beneath them.

I was now more akin to these beings who floated under the foundation, for I too, was a being under the water now.

And no different than how I saw their eyes when I once stood on the icy ground of the village, so too did these beings see *my* eyes looking at them now.

Just as much as they looked at me in that moment, I was looking at them from a similar position, which made me now a being in the water— a pair of eyes which swam beneath the surface.

And sure enough, after their brief glance and inspection of me— an acknowledgment, as I like to say —the gods returned their focus to the splashing waters above them, as the residents continued to enter their space for embrace.

Similarly, I returned my focus to the stars and galaxies beyond, and continued my swim towards them, for it was going to be a long long journey before I reached any. And while I swam, my awareness and being continued to expand and grow in an accelerated evolution.

… That is where I find myself now. And where I was also able to find you, as my consciousness gained insight unto your subtle presence, and a relation was found.

I hope this, my story, may help you. Or at the very least, will not go forgotten.

So many things about that small icy village make sense now.

What once seemed out of place is now viewed in whole as the perfectly shaped puzzle, finally finished and made into one image by the hundreds of little pieces.

One can never see such things fully while still inside the structure… less they have many eyes, which only four of my peers were originally blessed with in Gatsbahlburg.

I told you at the beginning of this story that I would share with you the full Prophecy at its end.

Well, now we are here.

Behold— the last piece of the puzzle. Something I had that didn't make sense for most of my life, and something you didn't have which would make sense of it all.

But never forget: the most important piece of the puzzle you can ever have… is yourself.

"Here we Pilgrims traveled. Here we Pilgrims unite. Upon the outskirts of chaos— life itself —the outer petal from what is the flurrying blossom of the Universe. We sought to escape it all. And so we journeyed to find purity. Purity in Peace. Purity in Nature. Purity in Breath. What is found, has been found, and to be found at the edge of existence is not our answer. Surely, this is not it. Where it lies— that which we seek —is within ourselves. And the outskirts of the blossom is merely the grounds in which we may now discover exactly so. For within the bud where pollen sprouts and flourishes, so too, do the buzzing of bees which hum a distraction. Speedy do, we too, become that pollen that nourishes the existence of life, the progression of space, the events of time, and

the evolution of being. Speedy do we become the bees and join in their hum. And speedy do the other critters, who are attracted to its center where the nectar rests ever alluring, come to feast on the affairs of our trials. To escape the center is to be free in Peace. Free in Nature. Free in Breath. And so, we Pilgrims sought the edge of the flower. Fools we are not, for no Peace is to be found here; no Nature is to be different; no Breath is to be final. But true Peace can be created; true Nature can be unfolded; true Breath can be experienced— when the bees are not buzzing, and the critters do not crawl about, and the hum is not mimicked, and the only thing that is effected by your evolution... is yourself. We are not alone. We are not the only pilgrims. We are not the only beings who crave that silence on the edge of the petal. There are others— different and alike, but always the same of heart. Ours is this slab of ice. Ours bears the Four Fruits. Ours have Her. Ours is Gatsbahlburg. Let us, who live here, go on to live our lives as exactly life is. Should we create harmony and peace, then let it be so. Should we fashion weapons and make war, then let it be so. Should we burn down the Four Fruits and sink into our own demise, then let it be so. Should we cast out all metal and any weapons we may make, into the ocean— to forever hold peace and never have the constructs of violence, then let it be so. Our resources, our actions, our lives, and our doings, shall be nothing other than our own. There are no bees here, there is no hum, there are no creatures or critters of the other, there is no influence or impression or guidance that touches our lives or pushes our direction towards any one way... other than our own. And Her, the great and powerful one who rules this piece of the edge, carries that same indifference which we believe in. She is neutral, and allows us such purity in our proceedings that will unfold reality to how we see fit— our own natural evolution and transformation. She leaves us to ourselves now... but She shall return. For even wishing to no longer be on the outskirts is a likely evolution and preference that many of us, few of us, or all of us may experience. She shall return, and Her glowing blue eyes will mark the new age of Gatsbahlburg. Only She shall know when, and only She will be the one to choose who will herald us into our next venture when we, ourselves, begin to buzz like the bees that we once wished to escape. And with that, Her choice will be made, and then will come ours. Her choice shall lead us into the new Gatsbahlburg, which is a return to the purist state of it which has fled us by our own making. And our choice will be to continue as the residents of Gatsbahlburg… or to find that our evolution and desire of the natural self-transformation has beckoned us back to the center of the pollen. For with this Prophecy I declare, I tell you all— live; breathe; be; follow your nature and your hearts; grow and flourish by which way you see fit; let it be your own; let it be by only us— good or bad; and let Her come again when we ourselves have lost sight of it all and what the outskirts truly entailed, should we ever start to hum— unaware of what such a thing is after successfully being away from it for so long. Hoist the totem up tall at the entrance, let us not forget this truth in the centuries that shall pass here. And let this Prophecy ring forever until it is closed, and only then may it be forgotten, as the chosen one by Her shall write the new one."

The End